Co

Under Fire

Facing Life's Challenges with Grace

A COLLABORATION OF
INSPIRATIONAL WOMEN WALKING
IN FAITH, COURAGE, AND POWER!

ISBN: 979-8-218-11955-3

Dedication

To every young girl and woman
who needs to be reminded
of their courage!

Contents

Acknowledgments

Thank you to everyone who encouraged us to share our stories of tragedies and triumphs. We did it!

Stephanie D. Douglas

Stephanie Douglas has a passion for the heart of the Lord and has been anointed to "rightly divide the Word of Truth" while teaching with power and authority. Her teaching is unique and easy to follow while her preaching compels you to want to give your all to the Master. She divides the Word of Truth unashamedly and without compromise.

Stephanie is the Founder of *Vessels of Honor Ministries, Inc.*, an evangelistic outreach ministry of healing and restoration. She is a sought-out speaker; being requested to preach and teach at churches, conferences, retreats, and seminars both locally and throughout the United States. Her passion is to empower God's people and teach them to live ***Up*** to who God says they are by dissecting the Word of God.

For seven years, Stephanie served as the Executive Pastor of one of the most influential churches in Long Beach, California, where she received both her license and her ordination to preach the gospel of Jesus Christ.

Stephanie has an earned Bachelor's degree in Christian Education and received her Master of Divinity, Christian Counseling in June 2022. Stephanie is also a graduate of Cottonwood School of Ministry and has completed course studies at Southern

California School of Ministry. She is currently working towards her Doctorate in Ministry (anticipated completion is June 2023). Stephanie has been honored with a Doctor of Divinity from Elbon Solutions College of Ministry and is a Duly Commissioned Minister for Volunteers of America where she serves as an Operations Manager and Chaplain for homeless Veterans. Stephanie is also a Certified Life Coach.

She has dedicated her life to the Word of God and is committed to walk in love wherever she goes. Her belief is that no matter where you've been or how far you've fallen, you **CAN** get up! God can take you from a broken vessel and mold you into a "*Vessel of Honor.*"

Connect with her on FB @Stephanie Jennings-Douglas

Chapter 1

I'M Bigger Than My Stuff

Pastor Stephanie Douglas

Saul was the first king to be appointed to the children of Israel when they were no longer satisfied with just the voice of the Lord through the prophet. They wanted a king like the other nations.

What happens when the call on your life is more than you bargained for? In fact, you never asked for it! It was thrown on you against your will. You were fine just "doing you". You were not running from it, but you certainly were not running to it!

Conflict speaks of incompatibility or interference of an idea, desire, event, or activity with another: it's a tug-of-war between your emotions and your will.

There are times when what we're called to do is in a tug-of-war with what we want to do.

In 1 Samuel, Chapter 10:9, we see that God changed Saul's heart, yet in verse 22, we find Saul hiding "among the stuff." Why was he hiding? I would venture to say that Saul felt inadequate to handle what God had just called him to. As most introverts, we don't always feel as though we have "the goods" to do what we see happening in our lives. Allow me to let you in on a little secret. If God called you to it, He's already equipped you to do it. Yes, it may take some training or coaching but the coach will only pull out what's already in you.

After Saul was anointed, there was a list of things that would take place and they would serve as a confirmation to Saul that God will bring to pass everything that the prophet had spoken.

One thing he was told was that he would come across a company of prophets and he would begin to prophesy with them (vs. 6). As the gift of God began to be demonstrated through Saul, some people saw the gift at work but began to criticize because of where/who Saul came from. Sounds very familiar. They said the same about Jesus… (Matt. 13:55, Mark 6:3, John 1:46). As Jesus began His earthly ministry, many doubted because he was the "son of the carpenter." What they failed to realize was that he was also the Son of God. As a matter of fact, He WAS God!

You will have those that will question your gift because of your past and who they think you are. You are so much bigger than your past! You're so much bigger than what you've done or where you come from. Can any good thing come from Harlem? Detroit? Compton? Jersey? Can anything good thing emerge from our current world crisis? I want to submit to you, reader, God specializes in bringing continuity out of chaos! He's not caught off guard when things around us begin shaking. Heb. 12:27 declares that the shaking happens so that the things that cannot be shaken will remain. When we ALLOW God to be free to do what

He do (colloquially speaking), we will be able to sit on the front row of history as it plays out before us.

The Bible declares that as Saul left Samuel that day and headed back home, God gave Saul another heart. Sometimes, you just must start moving. Once you start moving, God will begin changing and making things happen. Perhaps your heart has not changed about what He's called you to do because you have not turned from where you are or what you are doing. When Saul moved, God moved! He had to change Saul's heart because He knew that was not Saul's desire.

Has God called you to do something that you didn't necessarily desire? You may have had your own plans or goals about what you wanted to do and suddenly you find yourself wrestling between your will and God's will. When that's the case, you're not as quick to give God a "yes" even though you love Him and want to please Him. Most people won't admit that out loud BUT, He already knows.

God may change your heart, but your head does not always agree. Our hearts and our heads are not always aligned. Verse 9 said God gave him another heart. Yet, in verse 22 we find Saul hiding among the stuff. Your heart could be ready to do the will of the Father, yet your head will talk you right out of doing what you know is right. In Romans 7, Paul talks about the conflict between the flesh and the spirit. He gives the picture of the inner battle that takes place. You want to do what's right but continue to do what you know you should not do. Because of the inner battle, I find myself doing the very thing that I hate. The "B" clause of Rom. 8:18 says "For I have the desire to do what is good, but cannot carry it out" (New International Version). Contextually, the writer is speaking of sin. But we understand that can translate into a plethora of areas in our lives. In this context, we are speaking of when my plans are conflicting with the Will of God.

God sees in you that which you don't see in yourself. Saul did not see what God saw. There were underlying insecurities that Saul struggled with. Like Saul, if we don't grow past our insecurities, we'll never fully live up to who God intended for us to be. His heart was changed but his head wasn't. He had in him what was needed to fulfill the task, but his head wouldn't allow him to accept what his heart knew.

The mind is an immensely powerful force. It can be so analytical that it will talk you right out of (or into) the exact opposite of what's in your heart and then it will make you believe this is the right thing.

On Saul's journey home, he ran into his uncle who asked him what happened and what did the prophet say to him. Saul told him what Samuel said about the donkeys but left out the entire conversation regarding the matters of the Kingdom.

Why would he leave out this life-changing news? Has God ever said something to you that was so far out of your reach that you dare not share it with anyone else? Perhaps Saul was still processing the conversation. Perhaps Saul felt that if he just kept it to himself, God would change His mind and use someone else. Have you ever felt like that? I know I have. After all, who am I that God would use me in such a way? Well, I want to ask you a question. Why can't He use you? What makes someone else better for the task? Is it their education? Their pedigree? Their connections? I've taken out time to let you know that you are unique, and nobody can do what you do! No one possesses the unique qualities that you possess! You are the best man or the best woman for the task.

Conversely, there are times when God will show you/give you a vision that is not to be shared until it's time for the manifestation of it. You will have to hold information that the Lord is speaking to you. Saul did not reveal to his uncle what the prophet shared with him about the anointing on his life. When God's hand is on you, they'll see it without you saying anything. When the vision is from God, He'll surely bring it to pass. In the book of Philippians, Paul writes, "I pray with great faith for you, because I'm fully convinced that the One who began this gracious work in you will faithfully continue the process of maturing you until the unveiling of our Lord Jesus Christ!" (Philippians 1:6, The Passion Translation).

If only Saul could have gotten a glimpse of what God wanted to do with him. Perhaps his response would have been different. What about you? How different would your responses be if you knew the outcome? If we knew the end result, would we still need faith? I believe it's the unknown that builds our faith and produces the trust that we need in order to say "yes." Like anything, the more we do it, the more comfortable we become with it.

The people of God wanted to be like the other nations that had a King. Although they heard and were led directly by God (through the prophet), they rejected God's voice and asked for a King. Saul may have been one of them that was making the request. Little did he know that he would be the answer he was seeking.

I'm sure you are like me and so many others that are praying for God to do some things in the earth realm. Have you ever considered that You just might BE the answer you're seeking for? I know that was a hard pill to swallow. But think about the numerous individuals that God has used throughout history. Most of them did not come out of the womb knowing that God would use them in such a powerful way. But God knew all along. He told Jeremiah, "I know the plans I have for you." (Jeremiah 29:11, King James Version).

Although God chose Saul to be king, Saul never fully accepted that position. When it came time for him to be anointed in front of the people, they had to send out a search party. Because Saul was privy to that knowledge ahead of time, he decided to try and manipulate the outcome by hiding.

Please understand that our hiding won't stop the call of God on our lives. There was something you were born with that didn't need or ask for your permission. Whether or not you fulfill it is up to you, but you can't deny it's there. You may not be able to see the full picture, but the outline is there. You may just need to connect the dots.

Don't be afraid to walk into who God has predetermined that you will be. Even when you feel inadequate for what God is calling you to do, you will have to step out in faith. Feel the fear and do it anyway! (Susan Jeffers, Ph.D., 1987). You may feel small in your own eyes, but you will stand above everyone else when you are walking in what God has called you to do. It's something about fully walking in your calling that elevates you above the average. Please hear my heart. I'm not saying that you're better than anyone else. But I am saying when you accept who you are in Him, you WILL stand out because you're bigger than your stuff.

Write your reflections and takeaways:

Chapter 2
Triumph After Tragedy
Pastor Stephanie Douglas

"*So don't remember what happened in earlier times. Don't think about what happened a long time ago, because I am doing something new*!" *(Isaiah 43:18-19a ERV)*

After years of being enslaved, the children of Israel were free from their oppressors. The unfortunate reality is that their bodies were no longer the property of the taskmaster, but their minds had not been delivered.

Some of us find ourselves in the same predicament as the children of Israel. God has freed some of us from a traumatic season of our lives and yet the memories of what we were in continue to haunt and torment us. We can't seem to move past the memory of what was in order to move into what is.

My Story

When I was growing up, I was one of those that some would label as an introvert. It was just my sister and me and believe me when I say we were on the total opposite ends of the spectrum. She was loud and overt while I was extremely quiet. She loved to be the center of attention, while I found myself shrinking silently into the background. She lived her life out loud while most of my greatest moments were merely unrealized dreams that played out in my head.

After all, what did I have to say that someone would want to hear? I sometimes secretly looked at my sister and wondered, "how does she do that?" The thought of having that much attention on myself was inconceivable to me.

We grew up with both parents in the home. They would have celebrated their sixty-first wedding anniversary had my dad held on an additional eight months. Without a doubt, I knew my parents loved us! But it was demonstrated more than articulated.

I hated school when I was growing up! I would skip school all the time. Sometimes I would just get on the bus like I was going to school and ride it all the way around just to get off at the bus stop by my house and go back home.

It was so bad that I eventually asked my mom to check me out of my high school and enroll me in the continuation program so I could work at my own pace. I finished the 12th grade but didn't want to be a part of my graduating class, most of whom I had gone to school with most of my life.

It was at the continuation school that I met my friend Cheryl. One day, I let Cheryl and one of her friends convince me to go out with them. They came and picked me up; they were in the front seat, so I sat in the back.

We stopped at the store and grabbed some Golden Champale (y'all don't know anything about that)! We got back in the car and as we were driving down the street, we heard a horn honk at us. Within a matter of moments, we were being chased down Crenshaw Boulevard. Cheryl turned down a side street and we got trapped in a dead-end alley.

At nineteen, my life changed forever! Because Cheryl and her friend were in the front seat, they were able to run away. But me, I was not so lucky. By the time I got out of the back seat, the car I was in was surrounded by gang members, and they grabbed me and forced me into one of their cars. That night, I became a victim of kidnap and assault. I thought my life was over, but God had another plan! God actually used one of the gang members as an angel to make them terminate the plans that they had for me that night. What the enemy meant for evil, God worked it out for my good!

What I thought was the end of my life, was actually the beginning of my journey to becoming who I am today. Don't get me wrong, it was hard for some time, but I knew I was going to be okay when I no longer associated that street with my trauma. That experience was the catalyst to bring me out of the back seat of life and begin driving toward my destiny. It took a while before I was able to go past the area where the incident took place but once I did the first time, it got a little easier and a little easier.

I could have allowed the memories of what happened in that moment to define the rest of my life. I wasn't sure how I was going to get past what happened in order to move forward. At that time, I wasn't serving the Lord, so I didn't have the Word of God to fall back on. It was two years later that I would dedicate my life to the Lord.

Although I began to grow spiritually, I was still haunted by the memories of that night. I remember the first time I read Isaiah 43. When I got to verse eighteen and read "Remember not the former things…," I wondered within, how do I forget something so traumatic that still haunts me on a regular? I prayed and even went through a season of fasting because I wanted… no, I NEEDED to be free from the pain of the memory. It was during one of the fasts that I had an aha moment. I realized that the memory itself may not go away but it was the pain of that memory that I needed to be delivered from.

I was still lost and looking for the solution to get rid of the pain. As I continued to pray and do my intermittent fasts, I finally received my answer to how to get free.

I had spent so much time praying for myself but the answer to being free was my ability to pray for my perpetrators. Yes, you read it correctly! No, I didn't pray that God would strike them dead (even though I had days that I felt like that- I can laugh about it now). I prayed for their salvation, I prayed for their families,

I prayed blessings for the one that intervened on my behalf, etc. When I began praying for them consistently, God was healing my heart and I didn't even realize it until one day, the pain was gone! The sting was gone! The fear was gone!

This same girl that hated school, went back, and earned a couple of degrees, and multiple certifications, and was even honored with a Doctor of Divinity degree. I don't say that to brag, I say it with godly pride because I know who I was, and I am so grateful for who I am today and I'm even more excited about who I am yet to become!

Conversely, there are those of us that are trying to resurrect old things when God is trying to do a new thing. What you had may have been good, but God is trying to give you great!

Do you remember that break-up and how you thought you would never find another because it was the best thing you had ever experienced? But, had the breakup not occurred, you would not be enjoying the love of your life today.

How about the job you loved so much? You were devastated when it ended. But it had to end in order for you to get to the place you're at today! And anything else you may have experienced. Not all of it was bad. In fact, you've had some successful outcomes. You've won some battles. You've seen victories.

Please know that not every negative outcome means that it's over. Not every positive outcome means that you can't do it better. It simply means it's time for something new. God wants you to experience better. Better than what was! Better than what our finite minds can even imagine. The apostle Paul wrote in his letter to the Corinthian church, "However, as it is written: "What no eye has seen, what no ear has heard, and what no human mind has conceived"— the things God has prepared for those who love him—"1 Corinthians 2:9 (NIV). Stop tripping because it didn't work out! Stop trying to resurrect old stuff. There's a reason that is a part of your past. Leave it there!

I recently had to close the coffin to a project that I have had for years. Initially, I wanted to cry for several reasons. One reason is because of the time and effort that went into putting it together years ago. Another reason is because I felt as though I failed. I felt like God gave me a vision and I allowed it to die. I found myself trying to manipulate circumstances to try and resurrect it instead of embracing this season. What season? The season that Solomon speaks about in Ecclesiastes 3:6: "A right time to search and another to count your losses, a right time to hold on and another to let go." (The Message). It was time to let go of what was in order to embrace what shall be! I was so focused on what had died, I wasn't able to see that God wanted to bring new life, new vision, and expansion. John 12:24 says "Truly, truly, I say to you, unless a grain of wheat falls into the earth and dies, it remains alone; but if it dies, it bears much fruit." (ESV). It's through death that we experience life. It's through losing that we experience gain. It's through humility that we experience exaltation. "Humble yourselves before the Lord, and he will exalt you" James 4:10 ESV.

Let's take a look at our lives a little more closely.

What is it that you are holding on to that God is urging you to let go of?

What memory is still holding you captive? Perhaps you may need to shift how you are praying about it.

What area of success do you keep memorializing that may be keeping you from moving forward to what God has next for you?

After taking an introspective look at myself, my past failures as well as successes, I realized that I still had a few things to forget. How about you?

Write your reflections and takeaways:

Chapter 3

I Know My Plans for You

Pastor Stephanie Douglas

"For I know the plans I have for you," declares the Lord, "plans to prosper you and not to harm you, plans to give you hope and a future." (Jeremiah 29:11 NIV)

I recently obtained a Master of Arts degree in Theology. For some, this is an everyday occurrence. But for me, this was a dream deferred.

When we're growing up, we're told to set goals and to make plans. But what does it mean to plan? The definition of a plan is to arrange a method or scheme beforehand. It's taking a forward look and doing what is necessary to obtain the anticipated results.

As it related to education, my only plan was to get out of high school. I don't remember when or why the shift came but somewhere along the way, I really began to dislike school. I remember having a couple of friends that I hung out with in high school. We had specific days that we ditched school each week. After a while, I was missing more school than I was attending. I finally begged my mother to check me out of regular high school and enroll me into what they termed "continuation" school.

Here I am, this quiet, shy, introverted kid in a continuation school that consisted of gang members and other kids that were having serious problems, not just in school, but in life. Funny thing is, I didn't have any problems in school or in life, I just didn't like school. I never felt like I fit in. Once my mom checked me into the continuation school, I found myself wondering what on earth did I do?

It turned out to be one of the best things I could have done at the time. The continuation school allowed me to work at my own pace, in my own space, without the pressure of trying to fit in. As a matter of fact, it allowed me to get to know a population of kids that I otherwise would never have met. As I'm typing this, I'm realizing that that's where ministry started for me. I was able to understand those that most people misunderstood. I was afforded the trust of those that never felt like they could trust anyone. They found a refuge in me. I had no idea that God was using me even then. Romans 8:28 says that "And we know that in all things God works for the good of those who love him, who have been called according to his purpose." (NIV).

Not only did I finish high school, but I also finished ahead of what would have been my graduating class. It's not that I wasn't a smart kid, my struggle with introversion would not allow me to soar in an environment where I could not fit. I didn't know that then, but I've come to understand it as an adult.

Why is it important for us to plan?

#1- God is a planner… Jeremiah 29:11

There's nothing that God has done (or allowed) that He didn't have a plan for from the beginning to the end.

While science teaches that the world was created by happenstance; a Big Bang, our faith believes that this world was created by God in six days, and on the seventh day, God took His rest.

We believe that He planned out every detail. When you look at the intricacies of man and the fine details of our bodies from head to toe, you have to know that didn't just happen. When you examine our bone structure or the inner workings of our cells and veins and nerves and organs and tissues, etc., that didn't just happen. When you consider the brain and how various sections of the brain control certain areas of the body, no, that didn't just happen! We were created from a plan. Even when man strayed away from God, there was a plan of redemption in place that restored him back into right standing with God.

So, if God is a planner and we were created in His image, by all means, I believe He expects us to be planners as well.

#2- When we fail to plan, we are actually planning to fail.

I don't believe that people intentionally plan to fail. I work in homeless services. One evening while teaching a life skills class, I asked this question to the group that I was teaching, "As a child, how many of you planned to become homeless?" To see the look on their faces was heartbreaking! As the session continued, the common theme in the room was that most of them did not have a plan so unfortunately, they failed at life. A plan is simply forward thinking and strategizing on how to make it happen. Unfortunately, most of us just live from day to day, paycheck to paycheck.

What I realize is that a lot of people don't plan because they are afraid of failure and disappointment. Again, when we don't plan, our ultimate plan is to fail. You may fail a couple of times but that does not mean you'll never succeed. It simply means that you had a couple of practice runs while finding the right plan.

#3- It is God's desire to bless your plans.

"May he give you the desire of your heart and make all your plans succeed." Psalms 20:4 NIV.

A lot of times we're waiting on God to work on our behalf. Truth be told, we don't always give Him anything to work with. We have to have a plan in order for God to bless it. So, He's actually waiting on us.

Someone recently asked me, "if you had three wishes, what would they be?" I really didn't know how to answer that question. I'm so used to making it happen for everyone else that I very rarely think about what I want. I don't mean the day-to-day stuff, I'm talking about something that I can't, or wouldn't normally do for myself.

So, I pose this question to you. If God asked you what can He do for you right now, would you have an answer? It is my prayer that you plan and place it at the altar and allow God to bless it!

You may not always know the plan, but God knows His plans for you. When you find yourself searching for a plan, go to the One that promises to give you a hope and a future.

Father, we thank You that Your plans for us are to prosper and be in health even as our souls prosper. You know the plans you have for our lives. Help us tap into those plans so that we may succeed. When we find ourselves groping in the dark, lead us back to that place of clarity that we will find in your presence. In the name of Jesus we pray, Amen.

Write your reflections and takeaways:

Chapter 4
After This

Pastor Stephanie Douglas

"After you have suffered for a little while, the God of all grace, who called you to His eternal glory in Christ, will Himself perfect, confirm, strengthen and establish you." (1 Peter 5:10, ESV)

It was a Friday morning while sitting in a training class at work that I began feeling pain in my abdomen. While the pain wasn't excruciating, it was constant. I remained in the training with the hopes that it would go away but it never did.

When I got home from work, I called the advice nurse to see what could possibly be going on. When I finished describing my symptoms to the nurse, he calmly said, "I need you to hang up the phone and call 91-1." Although he was calm, I went into an immediate panic. But me being who I am, I did not call 9-1-1 because I felt good enough to drive myself to the emergency room.

Upon arrival, I was asked about my symptoms and then sent to get an X-ray and an ultrasound. They found a gallstone lodged into my liver. I didn't quite understand that since my gallbladder had been removed less than a year prior. I was admitted to the hospital and scheduled for surgery to remove the stone on that Monday. The surgery was supposed to take place in the afternoon, but I was taken into surgery first thing that morning, so I did not have the opportunity to call my family or friends; no one was given the opportunity to pray with me or for me prior to the surgery.

What should have been a same-day, out-patient procedure became a life-threatening, almost 20 days stay in the hospital. After the surgery was over, I had developed pneumonia, my left lung had collapsed, my pancreas was abnormally inflamed, my liver was messed up, my heart rate was through the roof, and there was an infection in my body that the doctors could not control. My numbers that should have been up, were down; the numbers that should have been down were up and nobody could tell me why or what happened. For the next fifteen days or so, I had multiple screenings and scans to try and determine why my organs were failing. They tried multiple antibiotics and none of them were working. I was losing weight yet swelling from all the fluids at the same time.

Another surgery was scheduled to find out what was happening. On the morning of the surgery, the Anesthesiologist came into the room to prep me. As he spoke with me, he was observing me. He stopped mid-sentence and said, "you're struggling to breathe, aren't you?" I said, "yes." He continued, "Ms. Douglas, I don't feel good about this surgery because if I put you under anesthesia, there's a great chance that you won't wake up." Of course, I told him to cancel the surgery.

Finally, around day 15 I began to turn the corner. My numbers started to stabilize, and I was finally sensing some hope from the doctors. But even though I was getting better, my heart rate continued to soar, and the doctors couldn't figure out why. I had a couple of false hopes of being released to go home. But because my heart rate was still elevated, the doctor would not release me. After a couple more days, although my heart rate was still elevated, it finally came time for them to allow me to go home. However, I was released with a heart monitor that was now a part of my daily wardrobe.

Still weak from all I had been through, I was finally home to start the recovery process. After being home for a couple of weeks, my family and I noticed something strange going on with my dad. He appeared to be leaning to one side and grasping for the walls when he walked. I asked him if he was okay, and of course, he told me that he was. I said, "No, Daddy! You're not okay! You need to go to the doctor to see what's going on!" He said, "if I'm not better in the morning, we can go to the doctor."

The next morning, dad was no better, so we took him to the doctor; they did a scan of his brain and the rest of his body. They found a mass in his brain and in his lungs. We were told that if he had not come to the hospital, he would have been dead in a matter of days.

They went on to inform us the mass started in the lungs and had spread to his brain.

My dad was scheduled for brain surgery. On the day of the surgery, he was in good spirits, and at 83 years old, he came through that surgery like a champ. He was up and talking within hours. In three days, he was back home with us. His recovery was going well! He was walking - on a walker - but walking. He was eating well, and cussing folks out (which was hilarious) … to know my dad, who barely even talked was now cussing folks out…it was so out of character for him. We figured the surgery tapped into some area where all this stuff stirred up. We got a good chuckle out of it.

Dad did really well the first couple of months, but the doctor suggested that he do radiation to assure that the mass had been completely removed and any other cells would be killed. They weren't really paying as much attention to his lungs at this time. He went through the radiation treatments successfully. Several weeks after he completed treatments, they checked to make sure nothing had spread to any other organs. At that point, it had not spread which was a great sign! Dad continued to progress, and we were hopeful.

He was scheduled to have a Zoom meeting with another oncologist. It was a Monday morning and we all sat around my dad and his computer. The doctor abruptly began to spew out all of these harsh, insensitive, unempathetic medical terms to my dad. She went on to tell him "Mr. Jennings, you will succumb to this cancer! I don't know how much time you think you have left, but it's not long!" She went on and on and as she spoke, I could see my dad's spirit begin to break. Until that point, we had never used the "C" word. As long as he didn't confess it, he was fine.

I remember asking dad how he felt about what the doctor had said. He got a little quiet and said he didn't believe what she was saying. "She don't know what she's talking about!" He lamented. We went on with our day. My sister walked with my dad and did physical therapy with him. He went to the backyard and checked on his vegetables that he was growing, which brought him much joy. Later that evening he had dinner, watched tv in his favorite spot for a while, and then retired to the bedroom. The very next day, everything in my dad had shut down. He couldn't move, he couldn't talk, he wouldn't open his eyes. Some time after he closed his eyes on Monday night, I believe that he reflected on the conversation of that day with the doctor, and it was more than he was able to handle.

We tried to care for dad for a couple of days, but it was too much for my mom and me. On Thursday, I called the paramedics to take him to the hospital. As they were wheeling him to the ambulance, I knew that would be the last day that I would see my dad alive. That was Thursday, October 1, 2020. Because we were in the midst of a raging pandemic, the hospital was only allowing one visitor per day. Since my niece lived up

North, we allowed her to see him on Friday since she'd made a special trip and my mom would go on Saturday. Before we could get dressed on Saturday, we received "that" call from the hospital, informing us that dad had passed.

We were devastated! I believe that part of the reason my mom grieves as much as she does is because she didn't have a chance to see my dad before he died. She didn't get closure so she has a lot of questions that we will never have answers to. My dad didn't like hospitals. The thought of death creeped him out. So, my mom keeps wondering if he was scared. Did he cry out for her? Did he know when he was getting ready to die? Again, answers that we will never know.

While still in the planning stages of my dad's homegoing service, my aunt, my mom's only living sister, was found in her home after having suffered a possible stroke. Almost one month to the date after my dad passed, my aunt passed. My heart was broken into a million pieces for my mom. She lost her husband of 60+ years and her only living sister within four weeks of each other. Mom and dad had celebrated 60 years of marriage a couple of months prior. Dad was her sidekick. They did everything together. She was lost without him. My continued prayer was that she would not give in to the grief. I'd look at her some days just staring into the atmosphere with a look of disbelief. Sometimes she had that look as if she no longer wanted to be here without dad. Sometimes she'd be sitting and thinking about her sister; her place of refuge that was no longer here with her. I can't help but replay in my mind the words that have fallen from her lips on several occasions, "you both left me" as if she wanted to be with them both and my heart breaks over and over again, feeling helpless. There are really no words for the grieving heart. So, every chance I get, I make my presence known. There's not a need that she has that I don't try and fulfill.

Slapped in the middle of my dad and aunt's deaths, one of my "brothers from another mother" passed. At this point, I'm just overwhelmed with life. My near-death experience, the loss of my dad, aunt, and brother all within a month's time. Not to mention several other deaths of good friends, I just became numb. It was the only way to get through each day without losing my mind. I shelved my emotions in order to care for those around me (word of advice, please don't do that. Deal with your stuff and then deal with others).

Let me pause and ask the question, have you ever gone through so much that you just don't want to pray because you don't think God is going to answer anyway? Have you ever been in a place in your walk with God where you questioned Him and wondered if it's really worth it? Okay, let me take it a little further, have you ever just been mad at God for what He allowed to happen? Don't judge me but this is where I was.

Several months after that, when I began to get my footing and started reaching out to God, my brother-in-law got COVID. At this point, my prayer game was back on, and I was believing God for His healing. I was quoting the scriptures for healing, believing God to lift him from that sick bed. For days we watched and prayed, trusting that he was going to be all right. There was nothing in me that even thought that he was not coming home. His wife and I would share every day. Some days were harder than others, but we believed God. Even after having a couple of setbacks, we remained hopeful. One night I got a call from my sis saying he had opened his eyes and was talking. We couldn't help but glorify God! We believed he was healing him to bring him home. Little did we know that he was having a lucid moment to say his goodbyes. Unfortunately, he went home to be with the Lord.

Here we go again! Really, Lord? His death really did something to me; more than I had let on. Not because of my relationship with him, but more because of my relationship with the Father. It's been a little over a year from my dad, brother, and aunt's passing and almost a year of my brother-in-law's passing. I must admit, it has been a rocky journey. It has been a fight of faith to get to where I am today. I recently had to ask the Lord, "Now what?" "What happens After This?" And He led me to this scripture (that means He's talking and I'm listening again- thank you, Jesus!).

I shared all of that to say, the God of all grace will perfect, establish, strengthen, and settle you AFTER you have suffered a while. I don't know what your suffering may look like. I can't tell you how long it will last but I can say with surety that it won't last always. It came to pass, NOT to stay.

As we look at this passage of Scripture, to understand it, we must look at it in context. Let's go back up and read verses 8-10. "Control yourselves and be careful! The devil, your enemy, goes around like a roaring lion looking for someone to eat. Refuse to give in to him, by standing strong in your faith. You know that your Christian family all over the world is having the same kinds of suffering. And after you suffer for a short time, God, who gives all grace, will make everything right. He will make you strong and support you and keep you from falling. He called you to share in his glory in Christ, a glory that will continue forever." 1 Peter 5:8-10 NCV. To paraphrase, the scripture is telling us to stay guarded because the enemy is coming after us. After being released from the hospital, I was not only weak in my body, but I became weak in spirit after the battle I had just come through. Because I was vulnerable, the enemy was able to catch me with my guard down.

In our text, we are admonished to be spiritually alert. Our adversary is aggressive and has one item on his agenda and that is to devour you.

In verse 9, we see that we are not alone. Have you ever gone through so much to where you felt like no one else has experienced this kind of pain? Although we may feel alone, the bible declares your brothers /sisters are also suffering or have been through the same thing. It may not be the exact thing, but pain is pain; it has no respect of persons.

After you have suffered, God promises to do some things for you. He says #1, I'll perfect you. In other words, I'm going to put you in order and make you who you ought to be. #2, I'm going to establish you. That means He's going to make you stable and turn you in the right direction that you should be in. #3, He's going to strengthen you; not just physically but He will strengthen your soul. The soul is the seat of our emotions, affections, and desires. It's the soul that deals with the pain and suffering that we face. And finally, He promises to settle us. He's going to put us back on a solid foundation. When we come through trauma, oftentimes our foundations have become rocky. But please remember, the foundation may have a few cracks, but it has not been destroyed. It just needs a little cement to secure it.

I was walking down the street and saw a crack in the cement. What amazed me about this particular crack was the flower that was growing through the crack. Although your foundation may be cracked, it's still able to produce something beautiful! My question to God is no longer "why?" My question now is, "what beauty are you going to produce *After This*?"

Write your reflections and takeaways:

Minister LaChera Thompson

Minister LaChera Thompson was born in Los Altos, California, the oldest of three children. She is the proud mother of three beautiful daughters, Ashley Antonette, Moriah Grace, Kaedyn Nevaeh and bonus daughter Shawntee Allen. She's also the proud grandmother to Zyon Keith.

In 1999, she relocated to Arizona where she worked for a youth outreach program as a group leader in an all-girls home. It was here that LaChera began to understand the call of God on her life and to develop a passion for young women.

In 2003, LaChera was ordained as a Minister of the Gospel at Long Beach Community Worship Center (LBCWC) under the leadership of Pastor Sheridan E. McDaniel. LaChera was always willing to serve wherever needed and thus served on many auxiliaries. LaChera also has a passion for prayer and has led several intercessory teams in and outside the church. To this day, praying for her family has been her number one priority.

It was at LBCWC that La Chera began dating the Sound Engineer, Keith Thompson. They dated for two years and married in 2008. Keith and La Chera's love and admiration for each other was evident to all and became an example to many others. The mantra they established prior to getting married, was, "Divorce is not an option" and they fulfilled their vows of, "For better or worse, in sickness and in health, 'til death do us part." on October 28, 2020, LaChera stood at Keith's bedside and held his hand as he took his last breath and entered into his eternal rest.

After the passing of LaChera's husband, she relocated to Grovetown, Georgia, with her youngest daughter Kaedyn, to begin the healing process through writing and journaling.

LaChera has made a promise to God and herself that she will not abandon the process of healing prematurely....no matter how long it takes and how uncomfortable it may be. She knows for a fact that when she comes out of this, she will be better and not bitter. She believes there is Glory on the other side of this, knowing that her pain is producing purpose.

Connect with her on FB@LaChera Renee Thompson.

Chapter 5
Grief and Loss

Minister LaChera Thompson

At the tender age of 14 years old, I didn't feel like myself; my energy was low and most mornings I didn't want to get out of bed and exhaustion hung around like a guest who had outstayed their welcome. Not realizing it, but the changes that were taking place in my body were the result of the life I was unknowingly carrying. You see, I was pregnant, and I didn't know it.

I can remember feeling scared, embarrassed, and anxious. The baby's father assured me that he was going to stick around and do the right thing. I never considered not having my baby, it just never crossed my mind. You see, I had friends that had already had babies. I was in high school, and they had resources for young mothers still in school. I had made up my mind and accepted the fact that I was about to become a teenage mother.

It had been well over a month since I had a period, due to the pregnancy, and my mother asked (out of that maternal instinct), "LaChera, when was your last period?" I knew at that moment I was in trouble. I was taken to a facility on Long Beach Blvd. to take a pregnancy test and to discuss my options for an abortion, no questions asked. Having my baby was no longer an option for me. I had been convinced by the people at the facility and other family members that I was just too young to have a baby. I was told that I would be making things hard for myself as well as this child. I was in no way ready to become a mother and it would not be fair to this child to bring him or her into this world.

The night before the scheduled abortion, I told my mother I did not want to go through with it and that I wanted to have my baby. She said, "make a list of the pros and cons of having this child." I remember going back to my room, grabbing a yellow piece of lined paper, and writing *Pros* and *Cons* at the top, with a line down the middle, and that was as far as I got. I cried myself to sleep that night. The next morning, I woke up numb, numb to the idea of having this child, and numb to the idea that I was about to take a life. I had decided that I was not going to feel anything because the pain I felt falling asleep the night before was the greatest pain I had ever felt in my life. I gave up the idea of having this child or any other child in the future. I decided at that moment I would never become a mother. I would never know if my child were a boy or girl as that baby's life ended after what would be the first of several more abortions.

After the abortion, I can remember thinking to myself, *I wonder what happened to that baby? Did the baby feel anything, was it painful? Did the baby somehow know I didn't want to do that?* These types of questions plagued my mind for days, weeks, months, and years and now and then, to this day, I still sometimes wonder. Then, due to what I had done, the nightmares started. I never told a soul, not even the child's father, who I was still dating. Well, less than a year later I ended up pregnant again and this time I lost the baby after just a few weeks into the pregnancy. Losing this baby was what I called a "secret relief." Like I said I was never going to have children. Little did I know or even my family know that after having that one abortion had become a means of birth control for me. I know this sounds cruel and selfish and inhumane, which it was. However, at that time in my life, I just didn't care. I figured if my own mother didn't care enough about the life in me, why should I care? Not realizing she was only doing what she felt was best for me at the time which came from a place of love, not from a lack of care and concern. For the record, my mother has since asked for my forgiveness regarding this matter, and I have forgiven her. This decision also affected her in a way that she too went through her own type of grief.

You see, grief is defined as deep sorrow, especially caused by someone's death. And loss is defined as the fact or process of losing something or someone. I was in such deep sorrow that I ended up pregnant several more times and each time ended with an abortion. Was I proud of this? Absolutely not! It was more painful each time I chose to do it, yet it was the only thing I knew to do. It was the easy way out, which is one of the things they tell you when you go in for an abortion, it will be easy and you won't feel any pain, it will be over in 5 minutes. They tell you, "You will be back to normal in no time." What they don't tell you about is the grief, emotional pain, and deep sorrow you will most likely experience after the abortion.

I suffered from nightmares for years, as well as regret, and secret resentment toward my mother. I never told her how much the abortion hurt me. You see, it was never brought up or even discussed once it was done. Everyone assumed I was ok, so I went along with it. I hated myself for my terrible choices and was too ashamed to talk to anybody about what I had done.

It wasn't until after the birth of my oldest daughter Ashley that I began to feel the pain of what I had done. Not only was I a new mother, but I was also a new believer and follower of Christ. Just seeing her beautiful little face for the first time, I couldn't help but wonder about my other babies, and what they would have looked like. How many were boys, and how many were girls? As I watched her grow and develop, I wondered about my other babies' personalities, traits, characteristics, etc. It wasn't until after I was saved that I found out abortion was a sin and boy did that take a toll on me!

There was no way I could ever forgive myself now, I hurt God! See, it's one thing when you do something and it hurts you, but to hurt God, that's another story.

I was a living breathing mess, ya'll. I wanted God to forgive me, and I wanted to forgive myself but the pain I had carried for so many years had become so deep and ingrained, I didn't know how it could ever not be a part of me. My pain and I had become one and learned to co-exist, if you will. It was a highly dysfunctional relationship because the more I wanted it gone, the more pain I brought onto myself. It wasn't until the age of forty-six that I was freed from the pain of my past.

I remember it like it was yesterday. It was a Sunday morning, and I was at church. Praise and worship had just ended, and I was up to exhort and greet the congregation and to read the announcements. As I stood on the stage, the praise team was finishing a song called "Break Every Chain." It was at that moment my mind went back to when I was 14 years old, and I began to feel the pain of that very first abortion I knew God had already forgiven me so why was I feeling this pain and why now when I'm about to address the congregation? It was at that moment the Lord spoke to me and said "It's time for you to forgive yourself," as the tears rolled down my cheeks and I lifted my hands as a sign of surrender to God, I forgave myself and instantly I felt as if a weight had been lifted off me. When I got to the podium, I knew I had to share with the entire congregation what had just happened and what was happening as I was speaking, God was freeing me of years of pain, hurt, condemnation and shame. Little did I know that there would be a young woman in the congregation that would come to me after service with tears in her eyes and say to me "You just saved my baby's life, I was scheduled for an abortion this week, but God spoke to me through you today and I'm going to keep my child".

Remember, grief is a deep sorrow and loss is the process of losing something or someone. That's exactly what an abortion is, and Grief and Loss are the result of it, not freedom or back to normal. In fact, it's the total opposite and the beginning of a long painful journey you could have never imagined or been fully prepared for. It's not even something you are always immediately aware of, and if you're not careful you can and most likely will find yourself picking up bad, unhealthy habits and doing things that you think will help you escape the pain of it, not realizing the escape you feel is only a short-lived one. Bad, unhealthy habits can never fully free you from grief and loss. It's an individual walk that you must allow God to take the lead on and the journey that must run its course. However, there will come a time to get free from the pain of it, and eventually you will be able to help free another. As believers, our grief and loss are never just about us and or for us, but God always has a way of using it for us and the benefit and advancement of those around us.

"Don't you see that children are God's best gift? the fruit of the womb his generous legacy? Like a warrior's fistful of arrows are the children of a vigorous youth. Oh,

how blessed are you parents, with your quivers full of children! Psalm 127:3-4 MSG

Write your reflections and takeaways:

Chapter 6
The Fingerprints We Leave Behind

Minister LaChera Thompson

Anyone who knows me knows I'm a clean freak. I'm not obsessed or anything, but I do like things to be clean, neat, and smell good. My husband used to tell me that was one of the things he loved about me-how clean I kept our home. He would always say, "I cannot wait to buy our own house so you can do whatever you want to it." He would also say, "I know you're going to make it perfect for us." Now don't get me wrong, our home was never Pinterest-perfect...lol; you could tell we lived in it. I was raised in a home where Saturday mornings were cleaning time and I guess that stuck with me. However, I've noticed since my husband's passing, I've been slipping in the Saturday morning cleanings. I have not let my house get nasty, but it hasn't been company ready at times. A lot of what I did, I did to bring joy and a smile to my husband's face. With him being gone, making sure everything was tidy and neat just wasn't at the top of my list.

Soon after Keith passed away, I noticed how dusty our bedroom blinds had gotten. I was so busy taking care of him, dusting was not a priority. I immediately noticed his fingerprints on our bedroom blinds and knew I was not ready to dust them away. Every Saturday morning, I would look at those prints and try to remember when he could have possibly left them. I remember one night so vividly. He heard someone in our backyard, and he woke me and said, "honey, somebody is in the yard." I didn't hear anything, so I said, "nobody's out there, babe. Go back to sleep." Less than a minute later I heard running footsteps and saw flashing lights and I said, "Okay, NOW somebody is in the yard!"

At that time, my husband had already become very weak in his body and could not stand or walk long distances without assistance. He kept a walker on his side of the bed for trips to the restroom in the middle of the night. That night he moved faster than I had seen him move in months. He jumped out of bed and sat down in the walker and peeked through the blinds. I, too, jumped up and said, "what do you want me to do, babe?" And before he could answer, the doorbell rang; it was the police. Apparently, they had been chasing a suspect and they shot him. He had jumped our fence and ran through our yard. When the dust of what had happened settled, I got back in bed and Keith stayed in front of that window and watched for several more hours.

The next day, we talked about it, and I asked him what he was thinking by jumping up so fast, despite being so weak. I asked him, "what were you going to do?" He said, "I don't know, but I was going to do my best to protect my family!" Deep down inside I believe that's why it's been so hard for me to wipe those prints away. To me they were more than just his fingerprints, they represented his love, determination, strength, headship, and protection he provided for us. He had no idea he would be leaving those prints behind and how much I would get from looking at them every Saturday morning. More importantly than leaving those prints on our blinds I can't help but think of the prints he left on my life. I am a better woman because of my husband, a better intercessor, and a better person overall. God used him to teach me so many valuable life lessons, such as what we leave behind in this world matters, the way we treat people matters, being honest matters and loving, even the un-loveable matters. I can do all things through Christ who gives me strength. (Philippians 4:13, Berean Study Bible).

Lord, help me to live a life that when I'm gone, my prints that are left behind will be worth holding onto because of what they represent. Amen.

Write your reflections and takeaways:

Chapter 7
Breakthrough

Minister LaChera Thompson

Way Maker, Miracle Worker, Promise Keeper

On the way to church this morning, I was experiencing an internal emotional battle in my head. In my mind, I want to be excited about going to church, yet I'm not excited. Not like I used to be. I want to be in anticipation of Praise and Worship, lifting my hands and singing God's praise, yet I'm filled with anxiety. Ever since Keith's passing.... church just doesn't feel like it used to. Don't get me wrong, I still love God, I still love His people and I really enjoy being around other believers.

People are praising, raising their hands giving God glory and I feel stuck. Stuck in my pain, trapped by my roller coaster of emotions. I want to sing, I want to raise my hands, I want to declare He's a Way Maker, miracle worker, promise keeper, light in the darkness because that is who He really is. Yet, I stand and listen - so desperately wanting to participate in the high praises to God, but I just can't. I imagine this is what Jesus felt in Matthew 27:46 where it reads "Eli, Eli, lama sabachthani? That is "My God, My God, why have You forsaken Me?" You see, I believed the miracle worker for a miracle, I stood on the promise of the promise keeper, and I looked towards that light on some of the darkest days of my life and at the end, I had to watch my husband die and that left me feeling forsaken by God, the one whom I trusted.

On October 28, 2020, I would stand holding my husband's left hand in both of mine, looking into his glazed-over eyes saying goodbye to him. His breathing was very labored and shallow. His grip was slightly loosening up. I could literally feel and see him slipping away right before my eyes. I told him how much I loved him, how much of a wonderful husband and father he was. How much I was going to miss him, how much I didn't want him to leave me, and how sorry I was for every argument, disagreement and time wasted being mad. I can also remember telling him how sorry I was for his sickness (cancer) and how sorry I was that his life was getting ready to end. I told him our girls loved him, his mom and dad loved him, his brother loved him, and all his friends loved him, and that God loved him. I told him how proud I was of him and the amazing fighter he had been.

There was a stillness in the hospital room the moment God came for my husband that I cannot adequately articulate. There was an equal amount of peace and pain at the exact same time that seemed to overtake me. I had never felt or experienced anything like that in my life and yet it was slightly familiar. God had stepped in the room to welcome my husband into

Glory and to comfort me at the same time. I would stay by his side for several more hours still loving on his lifeless body, still crying, feeling angry, let down by God, feeling forsaken. I hated it, I hated that I had to experience death instead of the miracle I so believed God for.

Eventually, I had to leave that hospital room and walk away from Keith's body knowing that I'd never kiss him again, never hold him again, never talk with him again, never laugh with him again, never hear his voice again and the list goes on. I was in a fog and couldn't believe he was gone. *Did he just really die? Did God really take my husband and hurt me like this? Am I being punished?* This is all a big mistake. I even made sure my ringer was turned on so that I wouldn't miss the call from the hospital later that night saying he was not really dead and that they had made a terrible mistake. These are some of the questions and thoughts that began to flood my mind.

So, for the next ten months, I would struggle in my faith, my prayer life, my praise, and my worship to God. As I said, I wanted to be engaged in prayer, praise, and worship but just could not. It wasn't until Sunday morning August 1, 2021, at New Life Church that something in me broke. The pastor's wife stood up and began to talk about this *Miracle worker, Way Maker, Promise Keeper, Light in the Darkness God*, and how we must declare that's who He is even when we don't get the Miracle we wanted. Just because we may not personally experience a miracle or the miracle we are believing for, does not mean He's not a miracle worker. It's not our realities that validate God's truth in our lives but it's His truth that gives us the strength to get through life's realities. She went on to talk about someone who had to watch a loved one die and yet they still chose to declare God to be a Miracle Worker. It was at that moment I felt something in me break and a shift in my perspective of who God really was and I was able to lift my hands and declare with the rest of the congregation that God was in fact a Miracle worker and Promise keeper and that He'd been my light in the midst of darkness all this time.

Grief and loss have a way of making you feel like God is not with you, you may feel let down and even forsaken by God, but the truth is that He will never leave you nor will He forsake you.

Write your reflections and takeaways:

Chapter 8
To Live in the Past is to Die in the Future

Minister Lachera Thompson

I was flying home from a trip and watching a movie titled *Tag*, featuring Jeremy Renner, Ed Helms, and Jake Johnson. There was a scene where a father and son were discussing the loss of the son's wife through a divorce. The son was still very angry and was rehashing the past when the father said something I felt was very profound, "To live in the past is to die to the present." I am not sure if this is a famous quote and I'm just hearing it for the first time or not. Anyway, as I'm navigating through the loss of my husband by way of death, I can see how this statement is very true.

Ever since I relocated to Georgia from California, all I've been able to think about is my life in California, before Keith died. I've even thought about my life in California before Keith ever came into my life. I've pondered several reasons why I should return to California. It rains too much in Georgia. My job experience was horrible. I don't like the Georgia humidity. The people are not like me. I don't like the way they dress. It's boring, I don't have any friends, etc. all the reasons to move back seem to be magnified. All my closest friends are in California, they are better drivers, The sun always shines in California…ok, not all the time, but mostly. I had a wonderful job. My oldest children are there along with Keith's family and so on.

When watching this scene and hearing the phrase, "To live in the past is to die to the present" is exactly what I was subconsciously allowing grief to do to me. It has a way of subtly, unapologetically crippling you to move forward. Keith was more than just my husband; he was my best friend, and he was me and I was him! When he died, so did a part of me. I've been somewhat stuck "living/existing" in the memory or the past of "us." Sometimes all I want is to go back to "Team Thompson," being Keith's wife, him being my husband. Living in our old house, waking up next to him every morning, praying together, laughing together, watching tv together, going to the movies on Tuesday nights, just doing life together like we used to.

In my heart, I know I can never physically go back in the past, but in my mind, I've never left. That's the power of the mind, that's the power of grief. You see, it's possible to actually live in the past and be dead to the present, right where you are, and not even realize it. I've been so focused on going back that I've not allowed myself to truly live in and see the beauty and possibility of where I am, my present.

It's not that Georgia is so bad; it's that California was so very good and the life I had with my husband was exceptional. The love we shared, the challenges we overcame, and the marriage we built were something to be proud of and certainly worth remembering. Like I've said many times before and will continue to say, we were not perfect, but we were perfect for each other! Our motto was, "Divorce is not an option," and we stuck to that no matter what we faced. Sometimes I get scared that I'll never be happy again, I'll never live like that again, things will never be as fun again, and nobody will ever know me the way he knew me again. Therefore, it's been comfortable to let my mind live in the past. However, after returning from my trip to California and then hearing this statement, I've made a decision.... I'm not going to live in the past.

If God be God and His Word is true, I have to trust His plans are to give me a hope and a future. His thoughts towards me are good and not to harm me. I have to be like Paul and forget those things which are behind and press toward the mark. Does that mean I must forget my husband? Absolutely not. Does that mean I forget what we had and just move on? Absolutely not. It simply means don't get emotionally stuck to the point that all you want is what you've had! God has a way of working things together for our good and that includes embracing your uncomfortable present as you move forward from your beautiful past.

I love you, Keith Cornel Thompson, and I will always cherish what we had together. And as I move forward into my future, you will be right here with me in my heart.

Write your reflections and takeaways:

Terriline Cleveland, Senior Pastor

Gideon FG Baptist Church

Terriline Cleveland, lovingly called "*Pastor T*," is a native of Los Angeles, California. She was born and raised in the church and accepted Christ at an early age.

Early signs of her anointing could be seen in her work in the Youth and Music Ministries. Singing, teaching, young people, and directing choirs were her passions.

She relocated to Arizona in 2006 where her ministerial journey became clear. …And while music is where she began, she followed the leading of the Spirit and was ordained in Ministry in 2013.

Pastor T served for 10 years as the Executive Pastor of the Gideon Full Gospel Baptist Church, under the leadership of Bishop La'Tresa Jester and in 2022, she answered the Call of God to serve as the Senior Pastor.

Her ministry includes music, humor, straight-talk, and most of all, encouragement. She seeks to lead God's people to see and seek Him for themselves, find joy in their personal relationship with Christ, and serve Him and others faithfully. Her joy is to impact the lives of others by encouraging His people with one song, one laugh, or one sermon at a time.

Terriline is the Manager of Crossroads OB/GYN and has been granted the privilege of spending more than 25 years married to Pastor Rovann Cleveland, Sr. Together, they have five children and five grandchildren.

Connect with her on Facebook: @Terriline Cleveland.

Chapter 9

The Courage to Forgive...ME

By Pastor Terriline Cleveland

"I – yes, I alone – will blot out your sins for my own sake and will never think of them again." (Isaiah 43:25 NLT)

Forgiveness is one of the MOST difficult things for the people of God to grasp.

Though we know that He WILL forgive us, we struggle to accept His forgiveness and we struggle even harder to extend that forgiveness to ourselves.

My first marriage began as a fairytale but ended in strife, challenge, difficulty, and bitterness (I'm talking about me). It broke my heart. It broke ME. It broke my mindset on how to deal with the difficulties of marriage. You see, I come from parents who, on the date of this writing, have been married for sixty-two uninterrupted years. Good years, bad years, years when they didn't think they'd make it, but they did. So, divorce was not a part of my vernacular, but it happened. ...And as Anita Baker put it in her song, Fairy Tales, "she never said that we would curse, cry and scream and lie. She never said that maybe someday he'd say goodbye."

When the reality of the demise of the marriage became clear, my salvation stuck, but my faith shook.

My salvation stuck – God never left me – but my unwillingness to forgive left me bound, which separated me from not just God, but from the truth and the reality of my "self." For all that happened, for all that was (and was not), for all I did (and did not do) forgiveness was necessary – and I learned that it wasn't nearly as much about forgiving him as it was about forgiving ME.

Who WAS this person I'd become? Who WAS this unsure, fully apologetic, shell of my former self? I was unacquainted with her; I didn't like her, and I didn't want to get to know her! She was angry and retaliatory. She was reckless and without discipline. She didn't think much of herself and at times didn't care about anybody else. While I understood her existence, I didn't LIKE her.

She was stuck in what happened. She was stuck in the hurt. She was stuck in the failure. It's not that her pain wasn't full-time, full-blown real, AND difficult; but that wasn't the WHOLE story. The rest of the truth is this: getting over what happened in the marriage was one thing, getting over what and who I allowed myself to become was another!

It was easy to settle on what they did to me; it was harder to focus on who I ALLOWED myself to become. I had to take ownership of WHERE I was and HOW I got there. It was a dark place. It was a place I wasn't used to being in. It was a place I didn't know how to handle. ...But it was at this point that the words to a song kicked me into gear: "Be grateful because there's someone else who's worse off than you. Be grateful because there's someone else who'd LOVE to be in your shoes."

Wait, I thought my shoes were terrible. I thought my shoes were useless and done for until I heard those words and I DECIDED to live! So, my brother, my sister – hear me when I say that the stuff that has happened, HAPPENED. It did…but that's not all and it's not over!

I found the courage to forgive and then I decided to let God heal my heart. I decided to let God release me from the bondage of unforgiveness for the things I ALLOWED in my life. I decided to go after the life God predetermined for me before the foundation of the world. I realized that He allowed me to go through the valleys of my life to show me who He is and who I am capable of being; so, I decided to follow Jesus to the destinations HE has for me, and what a ride it's been! I'm 28 years beyond the end of that marriage and like the lyrics Marvin Sapp sang, *I'm stronger, I'm wiser, but most of all, I'm better.*

My encouragement to you today is this: don't let failures and difficulties define you.

The courage to forgive yourself is freeing and liberating and WORTH IT!

Ask God to forgive you and receive that; then YOU do what the text says, "for my OWN SAKE, I will never think of them again." Brother…Sister, let it go and live!

Write your reflections and takeaways:

Chapter 10

Courage in Life's Dead Zones

Pastor Terriline Cleveland

And Jesus answered and said to him, "Get behind Me, Satan! For it is written, 'You shall worship the Lord your God, and Him only you shall serve.' (Luke 4:8 ESV)

I once switched cell phone providers from Verizon to T-Mobile. Verizon's pricing was sky-high, and we wanted to trim some of the "fat" from our budget. We were happy with T-Mobile's pricing but have found that there are significantly more dead zones in their coverage than we're used to. We never know when we'll hit one!

Sometimes we must work through the "dead zones" of our lives. Times when we don't know what to do, don't know where to go, don't know what God is saying, don't have any vision, don't have any direction, don't want to stay where we are – but don't know where to go.

We're in a place that isn't moving, isn't growing, isn't fruitful, and isn't helping. I don't want to give place to the devil, but I know that the devil is behind the dead zone of my hearing, the dead zone of my doing, and the even dead zone of my being. Yes, I have a choice – but I haven't exercised it because I don't SEE where I'm supposed to be or where I'm supposed to go. I know I'm supposed to walk by faith…and not by sight, but I've gotten off track. At some point, I'm going to have to DO something to get through this dead zone.

In the text, even Jesus answered Satan. The text begins with "…And Jesus answered and said to him." Occasionally, I have to open my mouth and find the COURAGE to speak to the things that are standing between me and my breakthrough. Between me and my next. Between me and who God says I am, and between me and MY understanding of what God has said about me. Please be reminded that the devil is going to be at the TOP of his game ALL day, EVERY day. Since that's true, I'm going to have to ensure that my game is on point, too!

For this, let me introduce you to the dead-zone praise! A praise that isn't hinged on what I see or how I feel. It's the one I pull out when praise isn't my first thought. It's the one I pull out when I don't want to.

It's the one I use when my tears silence my voice. It's the one I go to when I'm a deer in the headlights of my life and I don't know WHAT to do. THIS praise is the one that is between God and me. You might not hear it if I'm in *Hannah-Mode*, you know…my lips are moving, but my voice isn't heard? THIS praise is the one that causes a breakthrough. This praise is the one that shifts things. THIS is the praise that I keep in my back pocket for times like this. Yes – it's time to pull out THAT praise!

The text continues that when Jesus answered, He began with a command: "Get behind me" ...and then He called the problem by its name "He said Get behind me...Satan."

Now that I've pulled out my "reserve praise," I've got the courage to take COMMAND of what's going on around me!

I declare that what's happening in the natural cannot thwart what is happening in the Spirit. I command my life in the natural to bow to the plans He has for me; I command my mind to bow to the Power of the Spirit that is at work IN me. I command my body to understand that by His stripes I am healed in the Name of Jesus. I declare that the direction and vision for my life are being revealed to me day-by-day, by the Spirit of the Living God. ...And I declare that I am now sensitive to the voice of the Holy Spirit in my life; I can hear His direction clearly and my obedience will not fail.

But finally, Jesus declared that the Word of the Lord requires that I "worship the Lord my God and Him ONLY shall I serve."

While I fully acknowledge the dead zones we talked about at the top of the discussion, I'm so glad that as I worship God, I AM moving THROUGH this dead space, I am growing while I'm going through, and I AM fruitful despite the deadness around me. Because of the God I serve, I am alive to His thoughts, His ways, His will, and His Word.

...And because I worship Him and Him ONLY, I don't have time to SPEND on the devil's tactics. I worship Him and Him only, hence, while I'm willing to command the devil according to the Word, "get thee behind me," I've found the courage to walk away from his antics! I'm no longer a spectator waiting to see what he throws at me next. He can do whatever he wants because I'm clear that greater is He that is *in* me than the devil that is *after* me!

I thank God that every decision I make will become an act of worship. I thank Him for ordering my steps and giving me the courage to move forward. I thank Him for walking me through the dead zones. I thank Him for being the lifter of my head. I thank Him for the privilege of Worship. I thank Him for BEING my God. ...And I thank Him that I can present my mind, my heart, my soul, my will, and my body as a living sacrifice as my reasonable act of Worship.

I recognize that we hit dead zones from time to time, but I'm SO glad that He's enough God to get me THROUGH them. ...And I can recover my connection at any time!

Write your reflections and takeaways:

Chapter 11

The Value of an Enemy

Pastor Terriline Cleveland

"Now Judas, who betrayed him, knew the place, because Jesus had often met there with his disciples. So Judas came to the garden, guiding a detachment of soldiers and some officials from the chief priests and the Pharisees. They were carrying torches, lanterns, and weapons." (John 18:2-3 NIV)

I have spent many years operating in and around enemies and frenemies. As a young person, I was too smart, or too pretty (yes, I was both…). I was too light, or too short. There were a variety of reasons I was given for these enemies, none of which had anything to DO with who I was, or what I was actually doing.

As an older woman, my frenemies tended to hinge on position. Whether it is in my professional life or in Ministry – I've dealt with my fair share of enemies.

I've learned, though, that my enemies – all of them – have been instrumental in my growth and positioning in a VARIETY of ways.

They taught me to put my head down and block out the noise. They were instrumental in the increase of my capacity.

The increase in my capacity to love.

The increase in my capacity to stand.

The increase in my capacity to understand.

The situations my enemies put me in helped me learn to tame my sometimes-FIERY tongue.

In short – without them – I wouldn't be who, what, or where I am. My enemies were necessary.

Some of them walked with me for a long while before they revealed their true colors. Some of them had no shame in their game. They didn't like me, and they weren't SHY about that.

At some point, though, I had to decide whether I would lean into what my enemies were saying OR trust what God was doing.

Dare I suggest to you my friend, that people who aren't DOING anything don't generally HAVE enemies? Therefore, if you have them, you are – somebody! You are a force to be reckoned with. You are a mover and shaker in the Kingdom.

You're anointed for a thing that Satan DOES NOT want to occur on his watch! Let me show it to you in scripture…

Jesus chose 12 Disciples at the BEGINNING of His earthly ministry. One of those twelve was Judas Iscariot. Judas walked with Jesus, talked with Jesus, worked with Jesus, and both watched and participated in the things the disciples DID, yet we find in John Chapter 18, that he is the enemy that betrays Christ.

But forasmuch as we want to condemn Judas, I'd tell you that Judas was necessary!

They're at Gethsemane where Jesus went to pray. Prayer is the thing that bridged Jesus' trepidation about what was coming and His impending arrest. Prayer set Jesus up to do what was necessary rather than cut and run. Prayer is HOW we resist the devil such that he will flee (James 4:7).

As you live your life, if you take a stand for Christ, enemies will come, and opposition will happen. The kingdom of darkness will come for you, and they will try you. It's not wise, but they will try you.

They do not know who they're dealing with, but they WILL try you.

If they came for Christ, they will come for you! Listen…

In the hours before He LET the crowds turn on Him. In the hours before He LET them cry CRUCIFY HIM – Jesus FACED His opposition.

Not because He did not have the authority to stop the situation, NOT because He couldn't have called in legions of angels on His behalf…

He faced them because they were necessary for His success!

No Judas, no Calvary.

No Calvary, no crucifixion.

No crucifixion, no ascension.

No ascension, no Victory!

I'll say it again: my enemies were necessary.

Let me encourage you to see your life in balance.

Some folks don't like us because we rub them the wrong way. That's normal – we can't please everybody. We're not everybody's cup of tea, but...sometimes your proximity to victory causes your enemy to kick up a little more dust. Sometimes you've overcome everything ELSE he threw at you and the attack you're dealing with is the devil's last-ditch effort to knock you off your A-Game.

Jesus understood the necessity of the enemy. And we must understand this too. Don't push them away, stand flat-footed in the Power that is at work in you and do what God called you to! ...Be who He says you are. Handle the assignment. Overcome the disease. Get the degree. Beat the odds.

Don't get rid of your enemy. They're positioning you for your greatest victory! Remember: The God IN you is greater than the enemy coming AFTER you.

Man of God, Woman of God, you've got this IF you understand the VALUE of an enemy!

Write your reflections and takeaways:

Chapter 12

Divorce, Division and Multiplication

Pastor Terriline Cleveland

By the time we publish this book, I'll be 58 years old. I've been married for nearly 27 years and am happier than I can say. Life isn't perfect by any stretch of the imagination, but I promise – I'm happy!

This is my second marriage. What I'm about to say has everything to do with division, but please hear me when I say it has absolutely nothing to do with my first husband. He's a good dude. We (both of us) made choices that could have been better. We (both of us) chose to divorce. He is NOT the devil, so please don't lump him in with the bitterness often expressed by former wives of their ex-husbands. What I'm about to say is about me, not him. Got it? Ok…

Division is often the result of disagreement. Disagreement, when it cannot be resolved, when we cannot find common or middle ground, often requires us to separate from someone to move forward. This is often some of the most painful stuff we go through – but might I suggest to you that division sometimes results in multiplication?

While I often describe the most painful time in my life (divorce) as the blessing of my life – getting TO that place a) wasn't easy and b) didn't happen overnight.

It was the 90s and the divorce was final. I was still trying to "find myself" in terms of my career, my walk with God, and everything. There were things I knew, but as I look back at it today, you couldn't have PAID me to see what God had in store for me!

We were married for nine years, and toward the end, things weren't as good as I'd have liked. Then came the day we said out loud that we were ending the marriage. As painful as it was – it wasn't a fully bad day. Somewhere in the midst of the pain was an element of relief. So, we went our separate ways. Lots more happened, but that's another story for a different book!

I went buck wild as a result of the divorce. I had what I called a "good time" though sin was at the forefront of much of what I did. You get the picture...

I was in a GOOD church. I WENT to church every week. My Pastor literally lived down the street from me. There was Word all around me and though I heard it, I resisted receiving it. I resisted letting IT change ME. I was satisfied with the surface relationship with God, but I couldn't give myself fully TO that relationship because rejection messed up my mind, and full-scale rebellion was the result. I was ok with NOT having the abundance God promised in THIS life, I was ok with NOT tithing and invoking the financial blessings God promised behind the tithe, and I was ok with mediocrity (at best) and at times sheer low-life living.

Now, notice I haven't said ANYTHING about the idea that my ex-husband "did this to me" because the reality is that he didn't…I did it! He didn't MAKE ME turn to sin. He didn't MAKE ME doubt myself. He didn't MAKE ME rebel. He didn't MAKE ME do anything. The course of my life was what it was because "I" elected the "shine" of sin over the fidelity of faith. Questions? The truth: it wasn't him – it was me.

Now, fast forward nearly 30 years, and here's what I can tell you in all honesty.

The worst thing that happened TO me was the best thing FOR me!

The honest reality about ME that I had to face back then, snapped me (really it slapped me) back in line with God and led me on a journey to enlarge my territory from what it was then (just me and MY relationship with God) to the place where I now talk to people week after week with the WHOLE goal of helping them SEE God in their situations, SEE God through their tears, SEE God in their hardest times.

In Acts 15, Paul and Barnabas separated over a disagreement about another brother in the ministry. Their disagreement, according to the Bible was "sharp" – translation – it got ugly! And while on the surface it says that Paul went one way and Barnabas went another, if you look closely, what it ALSO says is that

Barnabas went to Cyprus and Paul went to Syria – MULTIPLICATION.

Had they stayed together, they would have covered one area at a time. Separating, though it was fierce, put the Word of God in multiple places at the same time! DARE I suggest to you that once in a while, it is the separations of our lives that cause the purposes of God IN our lives to come alive AND expand?

What if I told you that had that first marriage NOT ended, I wouldn't have met my Gurlz, and I wouldn't be a part of this project? Why? ...Because I met them through the church I went to AFTER the divorce.

Please hear me, I am NOT condoning jumping up and running from your marriage! Remember, I said I've been married to THIS guy for (going on) 28 years. What I AM asking you is this: what is hindering your forward progress in Christ, and what are you going to DO about it?

Paul and Barnabas reconnected sometime later – but their separation was NECESSARY at that time so that what EACH of them was to do could be accomplished. Man of God, Woman of God let me end this with a series of questions I had to face and answer for myself. Ready?

What has God said to you that you are not dealing with?

What are you holding on to that needs to be released?

Where is God trying to lead you that you're currently resisting?

Is it possible that WHERE He's trying to take you – is WHERE the blessing is?

Are your past experiences, difficult as they may be, catalysts for your future?

Can you allow yourself to see the blessing of your past pain? (It hurt, but it led me to...).

Is scripture true when it says (paraphrased) all things work together for our good? Or is that only true for other folks while you stew in your pain?

Divorce, in my life, was a TRULY painful BLESSING! ...But our greatest blessings are often realized on the back side of the trials and storms of our lives (ask Job).

My prayer for you – is that you have or will find your way beyond what happened to see what is happenING. When you do, you'll find God woven through all of the details of your life. When you finally SEE it, lift your hands, and tell Him thank you!

Write your reflections and takeaways:

Sharon Y. Judie

Sharon Y. Judie is an inspirational speaker and gifted writer, with several stage plays to her credit. Named "Playwright of the Year," a few years ago and recently nominated as "Best Director," Sharon's talent as a storyteller consistently opens doors for her to showcase her work.

She has authored two books: *Heart to Heart: Encouragement, Advice and Inspiration for Teen Girls*, an anthology of letters and advice from men to teen girls and, *MisLeading Lady*, an adaptation of her popular stage play of the same title. As a co-author in the bestselling novel, *Get Out of Your Own Way*, her story of confidence and perseverance encourages readers to walk by faith to overcome challenges.

After her husband's unexpected death in February 2021, she published the 30-day journal, *Love Never Dies, Learning to Live Again After the Death of a Loved One.*

Connect with her on FB @ Sharon Y. Judie

Chapter 13
Have We Met?
Sharon Y. Judie

When I was a little girl, my dad was my favorite playmate. I had a child-size stove, sink, and refrigerator that kept me occupied for hours at a time. I played well by myself but there was something special about spending time with my dad. When he came home from work, he would pretend to enjoy the imaginary meals I prepared for him. When I wasn't sharpening my culinary prowess using my miniature kitchen appliances, I used my dad's hands to learn how to give a manicure. Yes, my dad sat perfectly still and allowed me to use my crayons to color his nails. He would later share about the times he forgot to remove the color from his fingernails before going out to have a beer with his friends who gave him a hard time when they noticed my handiwork on his colorful nails. He was a trooper.

My dad had a rough start in childhood. He was the second born of four children and his father died before he was 10 years old. His mother would walk them to school and then return at the end of the day and forget how to get home, so they often slept in the park. Concerned neighbors called the authorities, resulting in his mother losing custody of them to the

State. My dad and his siblings were sent to live in an orphanage and in the 1940s, not many people were looking to adopt little children of color.

Occasionally, someone would open their home as a temporary foster home, but never long enough for my dad to feel connected or loved which every child needs.

Fast forward several years and my parents met, married, separated, and divorced when I was 10 years old, but my dad made sure he stayed involved in my life. I joined a softball team when I was in my early 20s and my dad came to every game. I played right field and didn't get a lot of balls hit my way, but my dad cheered for me like I was Babe Ruth.

When my kids were born, he became the ultimate grandfather. I've heard the best fathers get promoted to grandfather and that holds true for my dad. He would often say 'you can't give a child too much love.' Isn't that interesting? The one who was raised in an orphanage and in foster care and didn't feel love was intentional about giving extra love to children.

I'm fortunate to still have my dad. He turned eighty-five this past December but he's not the same strapping man who used to give me horseback rides. He has Alzheimer's and not only does he forget his own name occasionally, but he also forgets mine. Whenever I call him, he has trouble figuring out who I am, and he'll ask me who I am. I'll tell him, "I'm your eldest child." And with that said, he'll usually call me by my younger sister's name. I'll give him a couple of hints and I'll finally tell him, "This is Bonnye," which is my nickname. He always responds excitedly, "Hey, Bonnye!" Hearing him say my name makes me smile. A few minutes into every conversation, he'll inevitably forget who he's talking to and asks again who I am. You must have patience when dealing with someone with Alzheimers, so I lovingly tell him, "This is Bonnye," and he always responds like he's hearing me tell him my name for the first time.

When my siblings and I were growing up, my dad used to share stories about when he was in the military, or he would share stories about growing up in Kansas. He always had a story and my siblings, and I had heard each of the stories at least fifty times, but we would act like it was the first time. However, there were times when we'd tell the story right along with him because we had heard the same stories several times. Unfortunately, Alzheimer's has robbed my dad of his memory and with that theft went the stories he loved to tell. What I wouldn't give to hear him tell one of those stories one more time. What I've learned from my dad's condition is he's here, but he's not here. I've wondered to myself about the many times I've been in the same space and place with loved ones and friends but being somewhere else in that same moment. I had to repent, and I have to remind myself to stay in the moment.

Thinking of my dad reminds me that life passes quickly. James 4:14 says, "For what is your life? It is even a vapor that appears for a little time and then vanishes away." We may not know what tomorrow or the next day brings, but we can trust our Heavenly Father to walk with us through the highs and lows in our lives and in the lives of our loved ones. My dad's Alzheimers invades my thoughts as I wonder out loud if I'll face the same diagnosis. I have to reclaim my thoughts and bring those thoughts into submission and meditate on Philippians 4:6, which reads: Do not be anxious about anything, but in everything by prayer and supplication with thanksgiving let your requests be made known to God. Worrying about tomorrow takes away from the joys of today.

It breaks my heart to know my dad's memory will not get better, but I'm grateful for all the great memories we've made over my lifetime, and I'll keep those memories in my heart.

Here are some helpful tips for loving someone with Alzheimer's:

1. Provide simple instructions to your loved one so you don't overwhelm him/her.
2. Don't argue or try to reason with your loved one.
3. Try not to get frustrated or angry.
4. Find the humor in the situation if you can.
5. Relax your expectations and be patient.

Resources:

Alzheimers.gov
www.alzheimers.gov
Explore the Alzheimers.gov portal for information and resources on Alzheimer's and related dementias from across the federal government.

Alzheimer's Association
800-272-3900
www.alz.org

Write your reflections and takeaways:

Chapter 14
Straighten Your Crown!
Sharon Y. Judie

When my first marriage ended, I was devastated and confused. Marriage is touted as a lifetime commitment, so when mine ended, I felt like I had failed everyone, including myself. On a positive note, my ex-husband and I maintained a good friendship and we co-parented well.

In the wake of my divorce, my self-esteem was low, and I was convinced that I would be single for the rest of my life, but within a few months after my divorce was final, I met a man who seemed to be ideal for me. Like me, he preferred quiet evenings at home as opposed to going to parties and hanging out. I had always loved nature and being outdoors so when he introduced me to camping and fishing, I figured I had hit the jackpot. There's an old saying that I found to be true: If it seems too good to be true, it probably is. Not only were these words true, but by the time I found out the truth about him, it was too late.

At first, I found it charming that he wanted to spend all his free time with me, but I eventually realized it was a subtle tactic to isolate me from my family and friends. It wasn't long before my dream come true became my worst nightmare. Sadly, I had ignored all the warning signs of his irrational behavior and when I was finally honest with myself, I realized I was in an abusive relationship.

His constant efforts to isolate me from my family and friends were a tactic to control my environment and to keep me away from others who may have encouraged me to leave him. Fear can and will paralyze you and keep you stuck in a relationship that is detrimental to your well-being and fear is what abusers thrive on to stay in control.

On several occasions, I asked myself, "How did I get here?" I finally had to be honest with myself and the true answer was I had strayed far from God. I was ashamed to pray and talk to God and I couldn't hear His voice anymore; I didn't feel worthy to be in His presence, so I avoided Him. I empathized with Adam and Eve in Genesis 3:8: "Then the man and his wife heard the sound of the Lord God as he was walking in the garden in the cool of the day, and they hid from the Lord God among the trees of the garden." Why did they hide? They hid because they knew they had disobeyed Him, and they were ashamed, and I hid because I was ashamed of how far I had strayed, and I was ashamed of what I had allowed to happen to me.

It's in those times of vulnerability, the enemy will whisper, "Your sin has ruined your relationship with God, and He won't hear your prayers, so don't bother praying," but I am a witness that God not only hears our cries when we're in trouble, He is able to deliver us, and He's able to restore us and make us new! He did it for me and He can and will do it for you.

Whose report will you believe? Don't be fooled into believing untruths from the father of lies. Instead, embrace God's truth as found in Romans 8:37, which says, "We are more than conquerors through him who loved us."

If you know your worth and value, you won't settle for less than you deserve. Speak God's truth over your life and over your situation. You may not be exactly where you'd like to be in life, but you have to trust God to change your circumstance. You are His daughter, and He wants the best for you. You're royalty, my dear sister. It doesn't matter what you've done; it doesn't matter how long it's been since you've felt good about yourself. It doesn't matter how long it's been since you've acknowledged God or His presence in your life. He loves you unconditionally. He longs to hear from you, and He wants to shower you with His love, so hold your head up and straighten your crown and walk into your purpose and destiny. You owe that to yourself.

Reflections

1) Your past mistakes and missteps can be life lessons if you learn from them.
2) Remember your value. Don't lower your standards or morals to be with someone.

3) Set boundaries for what and who you will allow in your life.
4) Know when to walk away. It's better to be alone than to wish you were.
5) Straighten your crown and walk like the queen you are.

Write your reflections and takeaways:

Chapter 15
Expect the Unexpected

Sharon Y. Judie

What special day comes to mind when you envision a box of chocolate candy, flowers, greeting cards, and a special dinner? If you guessed Valentine's Day, you're right. Valentine's Day is typically a special day wherein married or engaged couples shower their significant other with gifts to commemorate the day. On the other hand, I've been told that many single people dread Valentine's Day because it magnifies the fact that they're a party of one. After all, Valentine's Day is the day for lovers.

I've always loved Valentine's Day, but my life was turned upside down on Valentine's Day, 2021. My dear husband, Carl, had been in the hospital for nineteen days and in the early morning hours of Valentine's Day 2021, a nurse called to tell me his heart had stopped. "If his heart stops again, do you want us to perform CPR?" she asked. "Restart his heart as many times as necessary. I want my husband to live!" was my response to her. She called back five minutes later to let me know his heart had stopped one final time and they couldn't revive him. "He's gone," she told me. I couldn't make sense of what she said. I heard her, but I never expected to hear those words in reference to my husband. In an instant, my life changed, and I was no longer one-half of a couple. I was now a widow. Truthfully, that word still leaves a bad taste in my mouth.

I felt like I was in a fog those first few days. I don't remember anything other than that early morning phone call. I often wonder if God protects our hearts and mind by allowing us to shut down, so we don't feel the full impact of the initial pain and confusion that accompanies grief.

Carl and I exchanged wedding vows in May 2002 in front of more than one hundred family members and friends. We had both been married before, but thankfully neither one of us was jaded by love. We were both in our forties and we both had adult children; we were excitedly looking forward to the next chapter of life. Thinking back now, I laugh about how we met. Carl's uncle was celebrating his 50th birthday and I was friends with the uncle and his wife. I had invited a gentleman to accompany me to the birthday party, but he had to cancel, and he couldn't come with me. As fate would have it, Carl was at the party. We talked that night and exchanged phone numbers. From that night on, we were together. I never asked if he was dating anyone and he never asked if I was. He was a perfect fit for me. He had a quiet and reserved personality and let's just say I was just the opposite.

Over the years I mentioned to others that I knew that we were going to get married from the very night we met. I didn't have a great epiphany. I didn't see a message in the clouds. Nothing out of the ordinary happened. I just knew.

We journeyed through life and did what married couples do: we worked. Paid bills. Traveled. Shared our hopes, dreams, visions, and goals with one another. We encouraged one another and we clowned around and laughed like little kids until our stomachs hurt. I fussed about him leaving the toilet seat up and he would fuss about me driving home by myself late at night, despite him suggesting I stop and get a room. We didn't always see eye-to-eye and we weren't perfect, but we were perfect for one another.

It may sound silly, but I never imagined living my life without him. We still had plans to fulfill, places to visit, and memories to make. During those eighteen days leading up to his passing, I remember praying and pleading with God and begging God to let him live; not for any selfish reasons, but simply because I needed him, and I loved him. I believed until the end that he would have a great testimony of survival.

We had planned to grow old together. "Eighteen years of marriage isn't enough time!" I cried to God. "Father, don't you remember years ago I asked You for at least fifty years with him? Please don't let him die!"

My husband's unexpected death has left a void in my life. We were both retired and happily spent every day together. We enjoyed one another's company. Not only did we love one another, we liked one another.

What's ironic to me is my last day at work was February 14, 2019. Carl had told me he wanted us to enjoy retirement together. On February 14, 2021, 731 days later, he was gone, but those 731 days were filled with so many happy memories.

A week prior to his passing, I had prayed and asked God for the opportunity to hug my husband on Valentine's Day. When I arrived at the hospital, he had already transitioned, but I was able to lay my head on his chest and hug him one last time.

I believe my life is in God's hands and although I don't know what joys, tears, triumphs, setbacks, and victories await me in the future, I do know God will be with me.

Reflections

Grief is the natural response to loss. If you've experienced a loss, make sure to identify healthy ways to manage your grief by doing things that you enjoy. Initially, you may not want to re-engage in any activities, so be gentle with yourself.

The best way to support yourself emotionally is by taking care of yourself physically. Identify what this looks like to you. I ride my stationary bike, walk, and dance for physical fitness.

If you feel stuck and need to seek professional help, do so. Being able to openly express what you're feeling can be amazingly helpful. Memorializing your feelings in a journal or writing letters and making a scrapbook of happy memories can also help.

Write your reflections and takeaways:

Chapter 16

The Best is Yet to Come

Sharon Y. Judie

Walking by faith has recently been a test of my faith. I have encouraged many others to live their best life and be all they can be. I had great advice for everyone, except myself.

A few years ago, I realized I was playing small and playing it safe. I had dreams about what I wanted for my future, but all I did was talk about those dreams without putting in the work to make them become a reality.

I was a slave to what others thought about me. So, unfortunately, I became paralyzed with fear. Fear of failing. Fear of not knowing enough. Fear of not being good enough. Fear of not being accepted. Those fears (and many others) kept me stagnant and parked in neutral, with the engine running but never moving forward.

Fifteen years ago, I wrote my first script. It was performed in my church, and the production was well received. Over the next six or seven years, I produced one play each year for my church, as well as other churches in the community. I was content having my talent recognized, but I knew there had to be more to my writing career than merely writing one script per year and waiting for the opportunity to produce a play.

I've been going to plays as far back as I can remember and after each curtain call, I would return home convinced my productions were destined for somewhere other than the four walls of the church, but I didn't know how to make it happen. I didn't have investors or deep pockets, so I wasn't sure how I would ever see one of my productions on stage.

Several months later my husband invited me to go to a networking event with him one weekend, and I agreed to go. We got up early that Saturday morning, and as I stood in my closet trying to figure out what I was going to wear, my dear husband casually mentioned that I needed to pack a black or blue suit, a white collared blouse, pearls, black heels, and pantyhose. My first thought was, "What kind of cult is he introducing me to?" My second thought was, "I'm staying home. Nobody is going to tell me what to wear!" Because I had made a promise to him, I kept my word. So, I reluctantly packed my suitcase with the "required attire" and made up my mind to enjoy the event.

We arrived at the hotel and the ballroom was filled with approximately 400+ people engaging in small talk. The excitement in the room was hard to ignore. We were given name tags and told to write our names and our dream occupation on the name tags. I wrote SHARON, Playwrite. Yes, the person whose deepest desire was to be a playwright didn't know how to spell the word. I wouldn't know the correct spelling until a couple of years later when a lady at church pointed it out to me – after I had five hundred business cards made with playwright spelled incorrectly. I proudly gave her one of my first business cards, and she called me later that night to let me know about the error. I thanked her for caring enough to tell me privately and not embarrass me.

When the event started, the gentleman facilitating the event was both magnetic and charismatic. His topic was Turning Your Passion to Profit, and I hung on to every word he said. The first day was long – ten hours of learning, taking notes, and engaging with others. I was learning more than I had imagined I would.

At the close of the first day, the host selected a woman from the audience that he would personally mentor for six months. He said he would teach her everything he knew. Her name tag had Business Consultant as her dream occupation. The facilitator, who believed in the power of replication, instructed his new mentee to select someone else in the audience to mentor for six months. She would teach and train her mentee everything she learned from the facilitator. Everyone in the room raised their hand in hopes of being selected. I was sitting near the back of the room, but I was on my feet, waving to get her attention, and she chose me!

During our first few calls, she dug deep to find out how she could help me turn my passion to profit. One of the first things she asked me to do was to stop saying, "I write plays," and to say instead, "I'm a playwright." She reminded me of the power of words. It was at that moment that I started to embrace who I was and who I wanted to be: a playwright. It felt like the scales had fallen from my eyes. I finally saw who I was and where I was headed, and I was excited!

Over the next few months, my mentor suggested that I join a professional organization for playwrights. I did my research and found one headquartered in Detroit, Michigan. I joined in 2013, and four years later, I was appointed to the organization's Board of Directors.

One day, my mentor asked me if I had ever considered renting a theatre for any of my future productions. I thought she was crazy. I questioned how I would pay for a theatre. She suggested I contact a few people whom I believed would invest in my dream. So, I took a deep breath and called four individuals I knew would support my dream. Without hesitation, they each said, "yes" and gave me money to rent the theatre. Let me restate this to emphasize the power in the words we speak: Those four individuals invested in my project.

The enemy will make you question all your decisions, so as soon as I signed the contract with the theatre, I began to wonder out loud if anyone would buy tickets. Mind you, all my other plays had been performed at church…for free. I was concerned whether those same people would now pay to see my play. My mentor reminded me to walk by faith, and for me to visualize that every seat in the theatre was filled. My debut production, Daddy's Girl, opened to a sold-out audience! Since that date, I have continued to produce my stage plays in theatres.

Over the years, my confidence has soared, and I no longer let the opinions of others define or design my destiny. I am running my own race and I'm not in competition with anyone else.

My life would probably have been different if I had not gone with my husband to the event that weekend. It was life-changing in a good way.

In case you're wondering why there was a dress code for the Sunday networking event that I mentioned earlier, the facilitator wanted everyone to dress professionally. He told us, "When you dress like a professional, others will treat you like you're a professional."

Since my husband passed away, I'm determined to honor his memory by accomplishing everything he and I talked about doing. I encourage you to revisit your dreams, visions, and goals because I firmly believe they don't have an expiration date. Trust God to help you achieve everything you set out to do. I'm encouraged by Psalm 27:13 (AMP), which says: "I would have despaired had I not believed that I would see the goodness of the Lord in the land of the living."

I encourage you to stay the course and remind yourself that you are worthy of having what you desire for your life.

Write your reflections and takeaways:

Elder Candace J. Metoyer-Simpson

Candace Metoyer-Simpson is a faithful member of ACT2 Ministries pastored by Bishop Andrew C. Turner, where she leads the Ministers and serves on the Board of Elders as well as the Instructor/Director of Ministerial Development. Whether in a classroom setting, or a sanctuary, Candace's love and passion for the Word of God is evident as she shares the Word of God in seminars, Bible studies and Worship services.

Candace previously served as an officer in the Pacific Baptist and Fellowship Baptist Districts as well as the California Baptist State Convention. In 2004, she was delighted to join the Executive Board of Sisters in Ministry led by Pastor Sonja Dawson. Candace is the proud mother of Joi Simpson who also answered the call to ministry, and they diligently work together.

Candace loves the Lord with all her heart and is committed to reaching the lost and seeing those who are bound set free through the power of the Holy Ghost. She is determined to serve and worship the Lord for the rest of her life, knowing that it is "in Him we live, and move and have our being!"

Connect with her on FB @Candace Metoyer Simpson.

Chapter 17
In Spite of Myself
Elder Candace Metoyer-Simpson

I grew up in an era where everyone attended church on Sunday. You could hear and see the hustle and bustle of the neighborhood getting ready for their Sunday Worship Experiences. In my household, my Dad would make biscuits, sausage, and eggs for us, after he shaved, showered and prepared for service - all while humming along to whichever gospel song or hymn was playing on the radio.

My Mom would be busy making sure that my brothers and I were dressed and ready to go. I loved going to church; the atmosphere was electric and exciting! I loved dressing up, hearing the choirs and congregation sing, and even the sermon. I got to attend Sunday School and see my friends as well as participating in many church activities. The church held a very important place in my life, in the life of my family (immediate and extended) and laid the foundation for my life.

From childhood through my teen years, I stayed active in the church, learning, and growing, and loving God. Now don't get me wrong, I was not the perfect never-do-anything-wrong girl. I went through the same phases of experimentation and boundary-pushing that teenagers and young adults go through, such as ditching class here and there, smoking, drinking, as well as sexual escapades. You would think that having a loving supportive family, doing well in school, and being an active and regular church attendee would be enough to keep me motivated and moving through life happily and fulfilled without a care. But not so. Between all of the experiences, relationships, interests, friends, and family that I had; I did not feel like I belonged. I did not feel like I was always accepted for who I was or that I mattered. To add to my mixed-up perception of myself, I did not think that I was pretty and could measure up to the other girls/ladies around me. I had low self-esteem, lacked confidence, and did not see that I was sabotaging myself. I had substantial and meaningful relationships throughout my life which included a marriage, I still felt lonely, unattractive, and unloved at times.

As we move along this journey of life, we will experience a lot of things that will bring us joy, happiness, and contentment. But no one tells us that we may also experience disappointments, despair, or be dejected from time to time. The narrative is once you accept Jesus Christ as Savior, you will no longer experience pain, problems, or persecution. But this is not necessarily so. Being a child of God does not exempt us from trouble, sickness, financial issues, divorce, or death. But, because we are heirs and joint heirs with Christ Jesus, he gives us direction, tools, and the fortitude to go through the journey. As we grow, develop, and mature in Christ and His Word, we are better equipped to handle the pitfalls, surprises, and troubles that come our way whether the enemy is attacking us or if we are suffering because of our own decisions.

As much as I prayed and studied the Bible to know His promises and His will for my life, I still fell for some of the enemy's tricks and traps, especially the little whispers telling me that I didn't measure up to the other women in ministry, or that I wasn't good enough; or I didn't have enough experience, or I wasn't anointed. The really good one is, "no one wants to hear anything you have to say." I would experience some growth and some victories, and then get hit by life challenges that made me want to give up and go back to familiar behavior when I felt comfortable and in control. The enemy will always distort the truth because he does not want us to discover our true purpose and destiny. He knows that once we block out the noise and distractions and learn to overcome our setbacks and insecurities, we will be victorious warriors for Jesus. The journey to overcoming the things that separate us and disrupt our purpose can be filled with a lot of unexpected twists and turns. If we are not careful, we will try to find solace in the behaviors, addictions, and relationships that we put behind us. We must carefully pursue God and block out the whispers, doubts, and temptations that come our way.

Because of my insecurities, loneliness, and low self-esteem, I found myself in a couple of sexual relationships including one that lasted over 18 months. While I knew that it was wrong, I felt at ease, I felt in control and mostly I felt pretty and desired. In fact, I only found security and esteem in sexual encounters. I was so twisted in my thinking that I didn't value myself or see any positives that I could contribute outside of these encounters. After some time, the relationship was exposed, and it ended in a painful way and caused hurt to several people. As I prayed for forgiveness and restoration, the Lord showed me several things: I did not have to hide behind sex to feel wanted, desired, or attractive; I had an addiction that I needed to be delivered from and He (Jesus) will forgive and restore when we sincerely seek Him.

Be inspired by the lyrics of Tasha Cobbs Leonard's song, *In Spite of Me*:

I don't cross every T.
I don't dot every I.
I've got more flaws than a little,
And I messed up a thousand times.
I don't always commit,
Sometimes I give up way too quick,
And then I get tired of trying to run away
From who I am to who I wanna be.
Some days are better than others

I can be up then I'm down.
But beyond my mistakes, I'm found in Your grace.
And this one thing will never change
You still love me in spite of me.
You still chose me, how can it be?
Every scar, every flaw, You see it all, You see it all.
You still love me, love me.
Oh, in spite of me,
In spite of me.

Write your reflections and takeaways:

Chapter 18

Called in Conflict

Elder Candace Metoyer Simpson

Have you ever wondered why so many people have struggled to become the leader, minister, or teacher that God called them to be? Many people desire the gifts, titles, and prestige that they think come with being at the forefront of their local ministry but struggle with connecting with the people that they serve. Many people may have a genuine desire to meet people where they are and assist them in becoming who God called them to be. Some want to work in ministry to either prove a point to others or bring attention to themselves. They love the exposure, the limelight, and of being relied on or their names being called on more than assisting God's people. When we fail to identify these traits, we are in danger of missing our true calling and forsaking our God-given purpose!

Called, chosen, and anointed to preach, teach, lay hands on the sick, and bring deliverance to the captives. Marital issues, bereavement, divorce, children who choose not to serve Christ, motives questioned, financial woes.

"YOU ARE NOW QUALIFIED TO SERVE"

Servant leadership is the paradox that says, *to be a true leader, you must serve.* The instinctive tug of the spirit man to press toward your destiny and be a person of influence, faith, and prayer; all while living with present circumstances. It takes an inward journey to unleash the servant within and discover that giving of yourself releases giving to you.

Where is your heart when it comes to serving others? Are you a leader (or desire to be a leader) for the perks and benefits? Or are you motivated by a desire to help others? If your attitude is to be served instead of serving others, you are headed for trouble.

Servant: Laborer, Slave, Bond Servant, A Worshipper, God's Prophet, Minister, Ambassador, Soldier, Messenger. Servant is used as a polite, humble reference to oneself ("Thy Servant").

Follow the ultimate example of Servanthood: Jesus – John 13:1-17.

Know who you are serving and the rewards: Matthew 6:24-34.

"The true leader serves. Serves people. Serves their best interests, and in so doing will not always be popular, and may not always impress. Because true leaders are motivated by loving concern rather than a desire for personal glory, they are willing to pay the price." (Eugene B. Habecker.)

"You've got to love your people more than your position," according to John C. Maxwell.

A Servant Leader Must Be:

- Adaptable to Change
- Able to Implement Change
- Able to organize and monitor a smooth transition success
- Wise
- Trustworthy
- Humble
- Teachable
- Faithful
- Prayerful
- Consecrated
- Consistent
- Accountable
- Responsible
- A Student of the Word

A Servant Leader Must Not:

- Be Envious
- Intimidated by Other's Gifts, Calling
- Seek Titles and Positions
- Cause Division
- Be Selfish
- Untrustworthy
- Be Puffed Up
- "Think more Highly of Himself than he Should" – (Diva Syndrome)
- Have False Humility

Jesus desires that we relinquish our agendas and plans so that we can become more like him by following his example while on earth. Luke 19:10 says, "The Son of Man came to seek and save those who are lost." ESV

Other words to consider:

1. Douloo (doo-loo) - Doulos (doo-los): Slave, to be dependent upon another. Self-Denial. I Corinthians 9:13-18
2. Diakonos (dee-ak-oh-nos): minister, servant. To set in order, to pursue. Voluntary service – side by side with a Pastor, Bishop, Overseer, or Elder. To serve with emphasis on the work being done and not on the relationship between Lord and Servant. Matthew 20:20-28

"Everybody can be great. Because everybody can serve. You don't have to have a college degree to serve. You don't have to make your subject and verb agree to serve. You don't have to know about Plato and Aristotle…Einstein's Theory of Relativity or the Second Theory of Thermodynamics in physics to serve. You only need a heart full of grace. A soul generated by love." -Martin Luther King

Write your reflections and takeaways:

Chapter 19

Strong Women

Elder Candace Metoyer-Simpson

Have you ever noticed how much time and energy we spend trying to solve life's challenges while everyone around us seems to be clicking on all cylinders? How do they do it? Their house is always clean and free from clutter. The children are well-behaved and polite. Their husbands are loving and attentive. They make it look like their volunteer work and ministry work is effortless, while you struggle just to get to church on time. It is these times when nothing is going right, it feels like God has forgotten you, and God is not answering your prayers. Frustration sets in and you find yourself yelling, "God where are you?" "Where is that perfect, great, life for which I have prayed?" "God, you said that I could have the desires of my heart." "You told me to seek you first, and I have been faithful to you and your Word."

You are not the first woman to ask these questions, and you will not be the last. So many times, women question their worth, importance, and the validity of their relationship with God based on what is considered "answered prayer." Even if you have not experienced the perfect great life that you dreamed of, it does not mean that you have done something wrong or that you are not worthy of God's blessings. We must not allow the things we see happening in the lives of others to be the measuring stick for our own lives. Know and understand that God created you in his image and likeness and you are exceptional, extraordinary, and empowered. Too many times, we women are ridiculed for a variety of things without realizing our worth and importance in the world. If we look around and consider everything in life consists because of women in various roles.

God has given women the capacity to have strength that cannot be measured by normal standards; women are strong in "soul" with the ability to bear calamities with fortitude and patience. Women can thrive through adversity, hardships, sorrow, and setbacks. Strong women can love unconditionally and exercise faith because of their connection with God. The Bible records many accounts of women who experienced various things that would have stopped the average person dead in their tracks. But God gave them the power to overcome negativity, sadness, barrenness, and health issues to become strong women that paved the way and set an example for many others. At the same time, we must be aware that the enemy is always roaming around seeking whom he may devour. His mission is to distract us from the goals and assignments we have; discourage us with continual drama and negative whispers; divide us with problems and failed endeavors that attack our faith and destroy our relationship with God because of weariness and doubt. I John 4:4(b) “greater is he that is in you, then he that is in the world.”

God gave me a simple prescription to use whenever I have found myself in a dilemma, in need of answers or help:

Pray
Persevere
Reap Prosperity

The first chapter of First Samuel records the account of Hannah who was the wife of Elkanah. Hannah had everything she wanted except a child. Because of this, she was severely ridiculed and teased. Elkanah loved her and tried to comfort her but nothing he did or gave her sufficed. Hannah went to the temple where she cried and prayed so hard that the priest took notice. Because he did not hear any words while seeing her mouth move, Hannah prayed to herself) he assumed that she was drunk. When he inquired about her drinking habit, she assured him that she was not drunk nor was she a person who drank wine. But she was pouring out her soul to God with her request. Eli did not ask what her request to God was but told her to go in peace because God was going to grant her petition. She was no longer sad and when she and Elkanah returned home, the Lord “remembered” her. Hannah not only returned to the Lord in prayer and thanksgiving, but she also gave Samuel back to the

Lord to serve him. We must commit to prayer on a regular basis believing in faith that God hears, He will answer, and He will bless us!

The portion of scripture outlined in Mark 5:21 begins with the ruler of the synagogue, Jairus. When he saw Jesus, he fell at His feet and asked Him to come and heal his young daughter. As Jesus walked with him, there was a massive crowd following them because the word had gotten around about who Jesus was and the miracles that He was performing. Mark 5:25-26 introduces the perseverance of an unnamed woman who had suffered many things through the various doctors that treated her with her blood flow for twelve long years. By now she had spent all her money and had no hope. But then she heard of Jesus and persevered through the crowd, the ruler, and all the people to touch the hem of Jesus' garment to be healed! The Bible says, *immediately she felt the blood dry up.* Jesus wanted to know who touched Him because His virtue and power had gone out of Him. She came before Him, trembling, and bowed before Him telling Him her story. Jesus declared that her faith made her whole. It took a lot of strength and perseverance for her to put herself on the line for a lifesaving and life-changing encounter with the S avior. She lost all her money, and doctors took advantage of her, but still, she pressed, persisted, and persevered. She went through severe life circumstances and experiences and God rewarded her perseverance.

The account of Naomi and Ruth is such an important example of God's providence and grace at work. Naomi and her daughters-in-law lost their husbands and homes and were left alone. As God led Naomi to leave Moab and return to her home, she instructed Ruth and Orpah to return to their families because she could no longer bare any children and they could get new husbands. During this time in history, men were responsible for protecting and providing for everyone. But Ruth did not want to leave Naomi and begged her to go with her. It was there in Bethlehem that Naomi taught Ruth how to work in the field of Boaz. Ruth caught Boaz's attention and he eventually married her. Naomi was blessed for God restored her prosperity, and her family name and counted Ruth as a daughter beloved who God allowed to prosper in her marriage to Boaz.

Strong women pray, persevere, and prosper. Strong women walk by faith, strong women exercise faith, and strong women push through sickness, heartaches, loss, grief, and disappointments. Ephesians 2:4-6 "But God, who is rich in mercy, for his great love wherewith he loved us, even when we were dead in sins, hath quickened us together with Christ, (by grace ye are saved;) and hath raised us up together and made us sit together in heavenly places in Christ Jesus.

No matter your age, economic standing, marital status, or educational attainment, be assured that God will restore missed opportunities and wasted time. Trust Him.

Write your reflections and takeaways:

Chapter 20
Encouragement through Life Challenges

Elder Candace Metoyer Simpson

We are currently living in a world that is very unstable, uncertain, and unpredictable. In the last few years, we have witnessed all types of drama, disappointments, and devastation taking place around the globe that has ushered in widespread experiences of despair, depression, death, and doubt. Everything that we see and hear in the news completely challenges us to stay positive, unafraid, and keep our cool while maintaining faith and trust in God.

Admit it, when you think about things that we deal with on a daily basis – family, career, school, finances, health, children, grief, etc. in addition to everything going on in the news; it is easy to allow those stressful and negative moments to overwhelm us and make us over analyze everything that can ultimately lead to bad or unwise decisions that will affect our lives. Instead of praying or seeking answers in the Word of God, we call our friends and relatives to vent, complain, and get advice when we should seek the one who is omnipresent, omnipotent, and omniscient. The enemy will use any tactic to distract us, discourage us and dissuade us. John 10:10 (NIV) says, "The thief does not come except to steal, and to kill, and to destroy. I have come that they may have life, and that they may have it more abundantly." The adversary, Satan, is constantly trying to sneak in and steal our joy, happiness, and relationship with God so that we are destitute, broken and alone. He wants to kill our will, our hope, our dreams and our lives so that we will not follow Jesus and bow to his will instead. His end game is to completely destroy our lives so that we cease to exist and begin to doubt that Jesus is still there with us, hearing us and interceding on our behalf.

You might be thinking *I tried having faith, I tried praying, I lived a life dedicated to him yet, my child suffered, my son was incarcerated, my marriage ended, I lost all my friends, I lost my home/car because I lost my job.* God has not forgotten us! He has not left us in the middle of life issues, circumstances, and situations to "fend" for ourselves. We must remember God said that He would never leave us or forsake us, and He will be with us until the end of time! What He is doing is giving us another opportunity to give our burdens and cares to him. What He is doing is allowing the everyday challenges and vicissitudes of life to draw us closer to Him that we may be fortified in the Word of God and in prayer and communion with Him. I'm not speaking of the "act" of partaking of the Lord's Supper as we remember the sacrifice that He paid by drinking "the blood" and eating of the "body" of Christ (1 Cor 11:23-30). In his book, Understanding Scripture, John

Piper explains it as this: Communion refers to God's communication and presentation of Himself to us, together with our proper response to Him with joy. Communion with God is the end for which we were created. The Bible says that we were created for the glory of God (Isaiah 43:7). Yet, glorifying God is not something we do *after* communing with Him, but *by* communing with Him. Many human deeds magnify the glory of God's goodness, but only if they flow from our contentment in communion with Him.

Because we are human and are subject to life expressions, experiences, and encounters, we must determine to seek Him in all we do and say, knowing that He is still calling us to have hope in Him, trust that everything we endure is working for our good, believe that even when trials and heartache come, and believe that He is a rewarder as we diligently seek him.

Usually when we see a beautiful butterfly, we look at it, admire it and go along with our day. We hardly ever stop to think about the transformation or metamorphosis the butterfly underwent to become so beautiful. First, an egg is laid on a plant (the plant becomes food to nourish the egg). Then it becomes a caterpillar which will eat and eat from various plants and leaves. It will split its skin four to five times as it grows to adulthood (while storing food). Once adulthood is reached, it will begin its transformation process and enter the Chrysalis – this is where the caterpillar is fully encased in a cocoon. It will stay in this state anywhere from a few weeks to two years. The cocoons are hidden under branches, leaves and sometimes underground. While it doesn't look like anything is happening from the outside, there is a whole new life being formed on the inside. Once the new life is fully formed and developed, it will break through the Chrysalis and be seen as a beautiful butterfly.

No matter what curveballs life may have thrown you, in any of those dark, quiet times you didn't hear from God or thought that you are alone it was probably during your Chrysalis and God was hiding you, protecting you, strengthening you and feeding you so that you could emerge victorious, renewed, revitalized and ready for the Kingdom work that lies ahead of you!

It does not matter what is happening in the world remember that you have a connection to the Life source, and He will be with you always!

Write your reflections and takeaways:

Made in the USA
Columbia, SC
13 March 2023

13618943R10078